SIMPLY WILD

The air was still. No music played in the background, no candles for ambience. There was only cool, clean air and conversation.

"Tell me something, Holly."

"What?" she asked, her eyes on his lips.

"How far are you willing to go with this relationship?"

"As far as it works."

Jake needed to confess the truth to Holly, but he was too selfish to do the right thing tonight. Her name became a sigh on his lips, as he pressed his body over the length of hers on the sofa.

For the moment, he held all the power. She was afraid, yes, but of giving too much of herself too soon. Daisy had been right when she'd accused her of choosing easygoing men for convenience. They were easier to control.

Jake wasn't the kind of man she could love for one night, then leave in the morning. Her own feelings were too intense for a brief fling, and he'd told her up front that he wouldn't be staying long. She wanted to be with him, bare and willing right where they lay, but not like this, never like this.

OTHER BOOKS BY SHELBY LEWIS

No More Tears

Simply Marvelous

Sacred Love

Simply Wonderful

Destiny

Sensation

Delicious

Published by BET/Arabesque Books

Simply Wild

Shelby Lewis

BET Publications, LLC
http://www.bet.com
http://www.arabesquebooks.com

ARABESQUE BOOKS are published by

BET Publications, LLC
c/o BET BOOKS
One BET Plaza
1900 W Plaza NE
Washington, DC 20018-1211

All Kensington Titles, Imprints, and Distributed Lines are available at special quantity discounts for bulk purchases for sales promotions, premiums, fund-raising, and educational or institutional use. Special book excerpts or customized printings can also be created to fit specific needs. For details, write or phone the office of the Kensington special sales manager: Kensington Publishing Corp., 850 Third Avenue, New York, NY 10022, attn: Special Sales Department, Phone: 1-800-221-2647.

First Printing: March 2004
10 9 8 7 6 5 4 3 2 1

Printed in the United States of America

Rosie, this one is for you.

I do not know what the murderer looks like, nor where he lives, nor how to set hands upon him.
> —The A.B.C. Murders,
> Agatha Christie

Prologue

Blue Springs, Arkansas,
early winter

There was a knock on Rayna Holdenbrook's front door. Single, she lived in a modern town house in a gated community, one that catered to successful business executives such as herself. She lived alone.

"Who is it?" she asked, her fingers tightening the sash of her lavender silk robe. Its hot-pink trim swung gently, the movement revealing freshly shaved legs. Beneath the robe, she wore Obsession perfume, nothing else.

"Tina."

Exasperated, Rayna flung open the door. "It's ten o'clock at night," she said. "How'd you get past the gates without me buzzing you through, anyway?"

Tina Nolan snorted in disgust. "That gate is a joke," she said. "One of your neighbors let me in."

Rayna brushed a lock of dark brown hair from her cheek. Her hazel-colored eyes were bold, her voice as angry as her stance. "It's obvious you need help. I'm telling Jake everything."

"That's what I came to talk to you about."

Rayna paced a few steps, then returned to her unwanted guest, more determined now than ever to stop Tina's harass-

ment. *"Why can't you understand Jake doesn't want you?"*
she said.

"He doesn't want you, either."

"My relationship with Jake is none of your business."

"Everything about Jake is my business."

Rayna shook her head in disbelief. "Jake doesn't know you're alive," she said.

Tina spoke softly. "That's what you think."

"Look," Rayna said. "I care about Jake. I don't want him feeling responsible for what's happening to you. Look at yourself. You're losing weight. You've got dark circles under your eyes. Coming to my house like this is wrong. This is the last time you'll ever bother me again. I'm pressing charges."

A knife appeared, as if by magic.

Too late, Rayna tried to defend herself. The knife struck her in the face, once, twice, again. She was struck in the shoulder, the neck, the chest.

In her final moment of consciousness, Rayna prayed that someday, somehow, the truth about what happened to her this night would come to light, the name of her killer identified. Only then would there be justice.

Yes, truth would be her sword, but who would be her avenger?

One

Jake Fishbone was the kind of man other men noticed, the kind of man most women gave more than a double glance. Wide shouldered and Chevy tough, he walked like a man who wasn't afraid of anything or anybody. He wasn't.

One woman had understood that beneath this powerhouse exterior was a man of integrity, that behind his keen eyes was a decisive mind, a man who understood that he alone was the master of his destiny. And that one understanding woman, Rayna Holdenbrook, was dead. Jake still found it hard to believe.

Every time he thought about Rayna, he felt guilty—he hadn't been there to save her. The guilt was relentless and it colored his world. In his dreams, he heard Rayna crying. Sometimes, he heard her scream.

In his dreams, Jake could pretend she was alive. He could pretend she might call at any moment, might stroll into his office unannounced and hungry for dinner. In his dreams, she made him laugh. But in real life, Jake couldn't bear to live in Blue Springs.

Angry that police were trying to pin Rayna's mur-

der on him instead of searching for the real killer,
Jake, in frustration, had lashed at the people who
worked for him, his family, his friends. Few people
trusted a man accused of murder. A man accused of
murder didn't know whom to trust.

Jake needed to get away from the incessant gossip.
So he had come to Guthrie, a place Rayna had never
been. He came to rethink his future and clear his
head. The best way to clear his head was to keep life
simple. Today, keeping life simple meant running an
errand for his cousin, Daisy Gunn.

The errand took him to Yesterday Is Here Today, an
antique lace restoration and sales shop located in the
100 block of East Oklahoma Street. The street was the
main route for town parades, which circled onto another famous street in Guthrie, called Harrison.

As he parked his Jeep Wrangler, Jake noticed the
owner of Yesterday Is Here Today, Holly Hunter. She
was juggling several packages and trying to open the
door to her business at the same time. He strode over
to help.

Holly watched him approach and stopped moving.
He was impressive to look at, a dominant figure so
early in the morning. His hair was dark brown and
shaved close to his head. His mustache and beard
were trimmed short for that barely there look. His
eyes were extraordinary, a dark gray and very clear.
But it was his lips that riveted her to his face. They
were firm and sculpted, a darker shade of brown than
his beard. He had kissable lips.

Men this hot didn't usually frequent her kind of
business, which was largely female-driven. Maybe toss-
ing and turning had shoved him out of bed and into
the street this morning. Realizing she was gaping,

Holly dropped the package perched in her left hand. Of course, he caught it.

"Allow me," Jake said, as he balanced the package with one hand and slipped the teddy bear key ring from her slackening fingers with the other.

"Uh," Holly said. "Thank you."

"No problem."

Everything about him was green light all the way. In Holly's experience, green-light men were disciplined men. When there was a job to be done, they did it. When trouble came knocking, they were the first to open the door. He was the kind of man she liked.

"Are you new around here?" she asked, hoping to get a conversation going.

"Not exactly."

Holly liked his voice. It was even and articulate, in a timbre that played with the pit of her stomach. The man had sex appeal.

"Just set that on the counter," she said, as she switched on the heavy-duty ceiling lights and fans. The atmosphere inside the shop was warm and friendly. Inventory was beautifully displayed in vintage furniture from Elk's Alley.

Holly normally didn't try to picture strange men naked, but this time she couldn't help herself. "What's your name?" she asked.

"Fishbone. Jake Fishbone. We have a mutual acquaintance, Daisy Gunn. She's my cousin."

Holly's eyes danced with shock. She and Daisy were best friends. Not once had Daisy mentioned him. "Well," she said, "I'm pleased to meet you."

"Daisy told me you have some lace for her."

"Yeah," she said, "I do." Holly wondered how a few minutes in Jake's company could feel this nice. His smile lit his face up, which lifted her spirits. She could only imagine what he'd do to her if he wrapped those mighty arms of his around her body.

She took her eyes off him to stare out the window at the traffic crawling by. Hardly anyone drove fast in downtown Guthrie, which meant busybodies like her other girlfriends had plenty of time to peek through her storefront window. Fortunately, Holly didn't see anybody she knew.

"Will you have dinner with me tonight?" she asked, impulsively.

His laugh was low and deep. "What time do you close?"

"Five," she said, willing her heart to be still.

"See you then."

As soon as he left, Holly ran to the phone and called Daisy.

"Hello?"

"Girl, girl, girl," Holly said.

Daisy's laugh was smug, as if she'd been expecting Holly to call. "Thought you'd like him," she said.

"Normally, I don't go in for matchmaking," Holly said. "But this guy is scrumptious, one of those gunslinger types. We're having dinner when I get off work."

"Cool. What about my lace?"

It was Holly's turn to laugh, a delightful mix of warmth and surprise. She couldn't remember the last time she felt giddy over a man she'd just met. "Guess I wasn't the only one who was flustered."

"Don't tell me Jake left without my lace," Daisy whined.

"He did."

"Well, well, well," Daisy said. "Holly Hunter meets Jacob Fishbone and they both get thrown for a loop."

"Fishbone," Holly said. "His name reminds me of Laurence Fishburne, the actor."

"I think so, too. Laurence Fishburne is so versatile. Good guy. Bad guy. Hunk guy."

"True, true. Want to know something else, Daisy?"

"What?"

"I really like Jake."

"Good," Daisy said. "My work is done."

At the sound of the front door opening, Holly looked up, expecting to find her morning clerk checking in for her shift. But it wasn't the clerk. It was Cinnamon Hartfeld, and from the look on her face, she'd seen Jake.

Rayna's killer contemplated the future as well. Two avenues were possible: one—do nothing, and hope that police would never figure out who murdered Rayna; two—do something, and hope to divert attention away from Rayna's murder investigation.

The killer opted to do something. After all, the stakes were life and death. The killer preferred to stay alive, even if it meant one more person had to die.

TWO

Jake felt uneasy, as if somebody were following him. If this was true, he hadn't been able to pinpoint any one person in particular who looked suspicious, but he couldn't shake the feeling he was being watched.

For tonight, he intended to keep things simple. Tonight, he had a date. Arriving promptly at 5:00 P.M., he strode through the glass door of Yesterday Is Here Today to the sound of bells ringing, a smile on his rugged face.

"Hello, Holly. How was your day?"

There it was again, that special combination of a man too intense to play with, yet too scrumptious to ignore. Desire crept into Holly's stomach, a yearning that stole a little of her breath away.

"Started off slow, ended up with a bang." Her flirtatious tone implied that he was the bang.

His smile suggested her womanly wiles weren't lost on him. He wasn't one of those men who considered women too mysterious to understand. Understanding simply meant paying attention to the details. "I suppose that's a good thing," he said.

Holly reversed the OPEN sign to say CLOSED, and resisted the urge to glance at her reflection in the window. She'd already checked her makeup and hair in a convenience mirror twice. The time for primping was over. It was time to enjoy herself now.

As she turned off the ceiling lights and fans, her stomach wouldn't settle, her heart wouldn't beat steady. If she died suddenly tonight, it would be during a period of pleasure. She wasn't nervous about this date, because she trusted Daisy's judgment and her own solid instincts. She was excited.

Jake represented the unknown. Within the unknown lay unlimited possibilities. She looked forward to the challenge of finding out why he kept looking through her window as if he expected someone at any moment.

"The restaurant is on the corner," she said.

If the evening turned out to be a flop, which she doubted, she'd have an easy getaway, since her car was parked out front. She could say a quick good-bye and be done with the evening and the man. Then, she'd call Daisy and tell her friend to mind her own business for the rest of their lives.

Jake found Holly's excitement infectious. He definitely wouldn't do much brooding tonight. He didn't expect a lull in conversation or many awkward moments. "Come on," he said. "Let's go."

The restaurant, a family-styled Mexican place, was only half-full. It was Tuesday, and the mix of diners ranged from a very young family to senior citizens and couples, like themselves. The environment was festive and friendly.

Holly was the first to speak, glad to know she sounded normal this time around. She was determined to make a good impression on him, as he had done with her. "Daisy came by the shop to pick up her lace."

"She told me."

Holly cocked her head to one side, a bird watching

the bird-watcher. "You aren't long on conversation, are you?"

"Pick a topic."

She figured she'd have to be very direct if she wanted info on this stud muffin's private life. If he wasn't interested in her, he wouldn't have agreed to their date. She tried a different approach. "I can't believe I missed seeing you at Daisy's wedding."

"I told her the same thing about you."

Holly was genuinely curious, especially since Daisy had been closemouthed about him. "So, what happened?" she asked.

"I missed the wedding, but made the reception."

Holly smiled. "I missed the reception, but made the wedding."

"Daisy's been telling me about you," Jake said. "The lace business was trumped up for me to pay you a visit. But my coming to dinner wasn't her idea."

"I didn't think it was."

"You sound sure of yourself."

She dipped a tortilla chip into a bowl of fresh red salsa. "You don't strike me as that kind of guy, you know, a pushover kind of guy. I figure you did it because Daisy is your cousin and you love her."

It was clear he appreciated her honesty as much as she appreciated his own. "That pretty much hits the nail," he said.

"You remind me of Daisy's husband."

"Kenneth and I look nothing alike."

"It's your demeanor," she said.

"Come again?" Jake trusted Kenneth, thought he was good to Daisy, but that was about it—other than the fact that both were large men who weren't afraid to get physical.

"You're both quiet," Holly explained thoughtfully, "kind of easygoing, but stubborn in your own way."

"Stubborn?"

"More than that, you're observant," Holly said. "I bet if you closed your eyes right now, you could tell me exactly how many people are in this restaurant, as well as where they're sitting, maybe even what they're eating."

"Is that right?"

"That's right," she said.

Instead of playing that particular game with her, Jake chose to pass the time discussing the oddities of their given names, and the teasing they'd endured about them through mostly happy childhoods. They agreed in the coincidence that both their names brought to mind Hollywood movie stars. The topic changed the stiffness of their conversation into a flow that produced laughter.

Their meal was served, large plates of enchiladas with refried beans and rice. The food was plentiful and hot, their evening together a success. They drank ice-cold margaritas in glasses rimmed with salt.

"Mmm," Holly said. "This is delicious."

She ate with relish, unashamed of her healthy appetite. She enjoyed a well-cooked meal. At home, she would set a place setting for herself at the dining room table, and light a candle as she allowed herself to make the transition from work to home. She would eat slowly, without the background noise of music or television, steering her thoughts away from her problems by taking the time to appreciate the home she'd created for herself.

By asking Jake to dinner, she'd opened herself to a different type of appreciation, the simple start of a romance. This was a man who didn't know about her childhood crushes or adult obsessions. This was a man who watched her as if it had been a long time since he'd been with a woman he admired.

He didn't stare at her with open sexual hunger, rather he lingered over her hands and arms and wrists, as if he marveled at their softness, as if he wanted to trail his fingertips over her bare skin. He could smell her, she knew, by the way he drew air when she leaned forward in order to hear him better.

Pleased with the meal and his companion, Jake felt himself relax. In Holly's presence, he forgot about Rayna Holdenbrook, forgot about feeling followed, and relished the prospect of learning more about the habits of his dinner partner. He liked her healthy appetite, evidenced by the way she steadily but daintily demolished her plate.

Jake signaled the waiter for more tortilla chips and fresh water, and to ask about dessert. Holly ate the chips and drank the water, but declined dessert.

"Daisy swears up and down I should weigh twice as much as I do," she said.

Jake cocked his head to one side and looked Holly over. "You're just right," he said. "A size six."

She paused, surprised by his sexy tone. Muscles, brains, and very observant, Jake Fishbone was proving to be a nice diversion.

"Close," she said, as she sucked in her stomach.

As the restaurant filled, and their meal neared its end, Holly spotted two of her regulars, one of them as big a gossip as she was herself. She wasn't ready to share Jake yet, not even for an introduction. This was her time.

"How about ice cream at Brahm's?" she suggested.

If they were going to have dessert together, she

wanted it to be at one of her favorite places for a special treat. She'd probably run into more people she knew, but at Brahm's, they weren't likely to stay long. It was a high-traffic restaurant.

"The one on Highway 33?"

"Yeah," she said. "Pineapple sherbet would be perfect for dessert." It wouldn't have as many calories as ice cream.

He nodded his head slowly, as if she'd scored another point. Not only did she enjoy her meal, she enjoyed many of the same foods he did. He liked an appetizer before dinner, followed by something sweet to finish the meal off.

"Pineapple sherbet is one of my favorites," he admitted. "It tastes light and goes with just about anything."

She grinned. "That's what I think, too."

Jake paid the bill.

Once they were outside, there was the sticky problem of getting to their new destination. "I'll drive, Holly, if you don't mind."

She liked the way he placed his hand at the small of her back to guide her from the restaurant to his Jeep. As she watched his butt while he opened the car door for her, feeling shy was the last thing on her mind. But why was he checking the street as if he expected trouble?

They wound up eating pineapple sherbet in a booth at the back of Brahm's Restaurant. The atmosphere was very informal. The sherbet was exceptional, made from quality ingredients. The evening had turned out better than a night at home with only herself for company.

"You know," Holly said, as she dipped her spoon into the sherbet, "I pride myself on having excellent information-gathering skills."

"Is that right?"

"It is," she said. "But in the two hours we've been to-gether, I can honestly say I haven't learned squat about you."

He relaxed his body against the hard back of their booth seat. His legs were sprawled beneath the table, his attitude that of a man who had nothing but time on his hands. "Ask away."

Now that she had his permission to be nosey, she wasn't sure what to ask him first. She'd assumed, be-cause of Daisy's maneuvering, that he was available, but maybe he wasn't. She wanted to know if he had a special woman stashed somewhere in his life. She wanted to know if there was a real chance they might become more than just friends. She had had enough of casual relationships in her life.

"What's your whole name?" she asked.

"Jacob Michael Fishbone. I'm the middle son of Jud-son and Hannah Fishbone. I've got an older brother and a younger sister."

"Age and birthplace?"

"Thirty-one. Blue Springs, Arkansas."

"Where do you live now?"

"Guthrie."

She almost dropped her spoon. He'd either arrived in town during the dead of night or he lived in the country somewhere. She now understood how tightly Daisy could keep a secret. She hadn't mentioned him to any of their mutual friends. If she had, Holly would have found out about him. She wondered if it was Jake's idea to keep his arrival hush-hush.

"You're kidding," she said, as she shoved the sher-bet to the side. "I mean, you aren't just visiting or something?"

"No."

Holly's mind scrambled for any scrap of news around town that she hadn't thought was significant at the time. The grapevine hadn't mentioned anything about this bodacious chocolate drop. That fact increased the level of mystery.

"Well," she said. "I mean . . . when exactly did you move to Guthrie officially?"

"Three weeks ago."

She put her elbows on the table and leaned forward. Three weeks was a long time for Jake to go unnoticed and for Daisy to keep him secret. "No," Holly said. "You can't be serious."

He laughed at the shock on her pretty face. Holly really did have a lot of nerve, thinking that because she knew his cousin, she knew him, too. "You are something else," he said.

"Well, this is hard to believe," she said, thinking Daisy must have enjoyed scheming for the perfect way to introduce Jake to her. It was like pulling off a surprise birthday party.

Obviously, Jake was skilled at blending himself into a small community, which meant he'd kept to himself. Unless he was doing all his shopping in Stillwater or Edmond, one of her friends should have spotted him at one of only two grocery stores in town or at Wal-Mart. Everybody in town shopped at Wal-Mart.

But then again, new people were constantly moving to Guthrie because it was quaint and quiet. The best camouflage was for him to carry himself as if he knew what he was doing, where he was going, and to keep his mouth shut beyond the simple pleasantries of hello and good-bye. This fit with her overall impression of him.

"Where are you staying?" she asked.

"Kenneth sold me his place."

Holly glared at Jake, half convinced he was lying. She almost wished he was lying, because it would keep him from being perfect. He was a home owner. He'd set down roots in a town where a kid could still be a kid.

"Well," she said. "Well."

Holly flipped back pages in her mind to the last six months. No, there wasn't any info in her mental data bank about Kenneth Gunn planning to sell his place any time soon. She copied Jake's laid-back pose. "Kenneth's house wasn't on the market."

"Private sale," Jake said. "No agent."

Holly eyed him the way she would a smooth operator, with a mix of caution and curiosity. Smooth operators were levelheaded men, the kind of men who didn't ruffle easily, who didn't back down from a fight that was right, or a threat that was lethal.

Jake was smiling, yes, and the smile was real, but it didn't tell her much. He'd mastered the art of talking for hours without saying anything he didn't want to say. His control drove her wild.

"Need any lace?" Holly asked, changing the subject a little self-consciously. She'd noticed that two of her regulars had spotted her. She still had some questions to ask Jake, but she felt she'd run out of time to ask them without being interrupted. It was bound to happen soon.

"Actually," Jake said, "I do need some."

"I was kidding."

"I rarely kid, Holly. I've got an old buffet of my great-aunt's that used to always have a lace runner on top. I was hoping to get the pattern duplicated from a picture. Do you think you could make it for me?"

"I can probably duplicate the pattern," Holly said. "But I need to see it first to be sure. Styles change dramatically over the years. I can give you an estimate on the amount of time it'll take to start and finish the project, if I take it on. A lot depends on how authentic you want the reproduction to be."

Jake was impressed. She let him know that she valued her services and that they didn't come cheap. He knew that it was sometimes difficult for artists to place a dollar value on their work. He liked knowing she recognized her own worth.

"Daisy tells me you're a specialist in your field," he said.

"She says the same about you."

"Raised here in Guthrie?" he asked.

"My whole life."

"Ever leave?"

"Not for long."

Jake suddenly realized Holly wasn't telling him much and he wondered why. Maybe there had been a hot romance that lured her away from Guthrie, but once it failed she returned home for comfort. "What keeps you here?" he asked.

Holly shrugged. How could she tell him that when she left home she missed her sister's red velvet cake on Sundays, her father's breakfast casserole made with fresh eggs from the chickens he kept, that her best friends were as unusual as their names—Cinnamon, Zenith, Daisy, and Spud, that she loved it when thunder shook the dishes in her cabinets and wind roared over the house? She treasured the red dirt of home, the wide untamed spaces, the bumpy roads, and the smell of honeysuckle growing wild. For her, this was paradise.

"Oh," she said, "I suppose I stay for the usual reasons, family, friends. You know. Same old, same old."

"Gotta be more to it."

Holly wondered why Jake looked at her so carefully, as if her response were truly important, not merely small talk. She cast her eye toward the exit. "I suppose it always is," she said.

She wasn't about to tell him about the bonehead she'd followed all the way to Oregon, thinking he was going to marry her. Besides, Bonehead was past history. Jake Fishbone was present history.

She switched the subject back to him. He was the one with all the secrets. He was the one who'd slipped into town when she and her friends weren't looking. "Why did you buy Kenneth's place?"

"I like being close to a large city while surrounded by a small town atmosphere."

"I like it too," she said, nodding her head as she warmed to the subject, "like knowing every other driver on the road, or making small talk at cash registers."

"Don't forget the weather," Jake said.

"What do you mean?"

"It's mostly hot when it's supposed to be hot, cold when it's supposed to be cold. Each season has its chance to do its thing."

"Then there's the open country," she said. "The ranches and farms, the rolling hills, the scarlet trees in the fall, the bright oranges, soft yellows, the way Guthrie really gets into the holiday spirit."

Jake nodded. "But I especially like Guthrie in winter."

Holly's face turned soft and dreamy at the idea of winter in Guthrie. "All the lights on the old buildings, the horse-drawn carriages, the people walking the streets in Victorian clothes, the annual Christmas walk where stores feature live entertainment and vendors keep their doors open late at night."

"What I like best is the way Guthrie looks after a snowfall," he said. "I always feel like I'm part of a postcard. Now that I'm here, I feel like I live in Mayberry."

She laughed. "Me too."

He stretched his arms across the table in order to clasp her hands. Holly was wonderful company, and yet he had trouble on his mind, trouble he couldn't share. Still, he couldn't pretend he wished he'd never met her.

"I want to see you again," he said. "Tomorrow."

"Yes."

She'd noticed the way his face had turned serious, his tone a shade deeper. There were layers to this man. A month of tomorrows might not be enough time to get to the bottom of him.

"I'd like that," she said. "I'd like that a lot."

Three

Jake arrived at Holly's single-story home on time. The air outside smelled faintly of burning wood. The sun sparkled against the blue-green gazing ball mounted on a faux marble pedestal in her neighbor's yard. Wind chimes tinkled from a nearby silver maple tree. Her yellow and white house was charming.

Jake parked his Jeep on the street in front. He planned to throw himself into the next several hours, so that his mind wasn't split between two women, one living, one dead. Rayna seldom left his thoughts. He revisited the good times they'd shared, the highlights of their friendship. She'd been one of the constants in his workaholic life.

The night Rayna was killed, Jake had been thinking about her, but had been caught up in his work that evening and hadn't called her. A hundred times since, he wished he had. He wondered if, in her terror, she'd been thinking of him, hoping he'd rescue her.

He'd never know, a thought that haunted him still, perhaps even forever. If only he hadn't put work before friendship. If only he had a second chance. If only he could accept her death. But he couldn't. He never would.

Jake put his thoughts aside. Holly's act was together.

She had her own business, her own home, her own life. She didn't need anything from him, other than companionship. It was all he could offer her, at least for now.

He hoped Daisy's silence about his connection to a homicide wouldn't ruin her friendship with Holly. It was a powerful, potentially destructive secret, a dangerous game he and the Gunns played.

He didn't blame those who doubted his innocence. There had been no evidence to suggest he was in any danger, either before or after Rayna was killed, so who would believe him? No one. Rather, he suspected, the police would think that he was trying to shift their investigation away from him.

As time wore on, and no killer was found, his credibility lessened even further. He was surprised how little his reputation meant once the Blue Springs police began their investigation of him.

What was a man if his name diminished in value day after day? An outcast. Close friends were supportive but wary. Casual friends were distant. Everyone second-guessed him. Could he be trusted? Should he be free?

Inside the house, Holly heard him cut the engine to his Jeep. She willed herself to wait until Jake knocked before she opened the door.

At the sound of his knuckles against the door, she waited a few seconds before flinging it wide, a smile of welcome on her face. This was a real date, one that had nothing to do with Daisy. She and Jake were together because they wanted to be.

"These are for you," he said, offering the flowers, which she took with a soft smile of appreciation.

"Stargazer lilies are my favorites," she said. "How'd you know?"

Even though he'd purchased the flowers from Daisy, the choice had been his own. "You just don't strike me as a rose kind of person."

Holly stared into his handsome face and knew that his gift was a serious gesture. She felt shivery inside. "Come in," she invited. "I'll put these in a vase."

As she hurried about her task, he looked around. Her place was small but cozy. Nothing shouted. This was a well-tended home that wasn't designed for show. It was decorated with comfort in mind. Jake felt he could relax here, breathe here. This was definitely a step in the right direction—forward.

"Your home is nothing like your business," he said, as Holly set the vase down. "I suppose I expected to find more of the same."

"Only when it comes to the clutter."

"The print on your furniture is busy, but that's all. There aren't any pictures on your walls, no books, but lots of magazines, and no television."

"You sound surprised."

"I guess I am. Your shop is done in dark colors, with reds for accents, but this place is the opposite, green is an accent instead of red."

Holly invited him to sit down, which he did.

"I come home to rest," she said. "There's a TV in my bedroom, but I get enough of talking and listening to people talk all day at work. I thumb through magazines to relax, and listen to music for company. Basically, I prefer to veg out when I'm home."

"I can understand that."

Holly had been alone with a man in her house before, but she couldn't remember ever being this turned on, this soon. If she was a wreck before he knocked on the door, she was really a mess now. She had butterflies—something special was happening here.

She smoothed a hand over her thighs. She toyed with the gold necklace at her throat, the diamond pendant peeking out from the collar of her blouse. Why had Daisy kept him a secret? Why did she still refuse to go into detail about him, other than to say that Jake was someone Holly could trust?

"How many bedrooms?" he asked.

Holly's fingers fell away from the diamond teardrop at her left ear. "What kind of question is that?"

"A simple one. I've learned it's not easy to figure out the size of a house around Guthrie by the way it looks on the outside. I wondered if your house has three bedrooms or two, and if it has a cellar or a basement."

Because Daisy was keeping her mouth shut about him, for Holly, Jake was a man with no past. Living where she did, in a place where few people were strangers, a man with no past was unique.

"There are two bedrooms," she said, "this main living area, one bath, a kitchen, a screened porch out back. I own the house."

"I can tell. The pride shows in your voice."

There it was again, that million-dollar smile that caused her stomach to do somersaults. "Don't you miss the action of a bigger city?" she asked. "Starbucks? Barnes & Noble?"

"A man can relax here, Holly, focus," Jake said, as he sat beside her on the sofa.

It was tough for Holly to keep things light and easy. She couldn't pretend they didn't have strong chemistry. She sensed that in his own good time Jake would tell her why he was hiding out at Kenneth's old place. For once in her life, she didn't mind waiting. There was a quality about Jake that made it feel as if her patience would be rewarded.

"And what are you focused on?" she asked.

"My sabbatical. I'm on a hiatus."

"From what?"

He leaned forward, his legs spread apart, elbows against his thighs, chin propped on his fingertips. He looked solid and strong, dependable. "I own a manufacturing business that makes birdhouses."

Holly was stunned. If Jake was who she suspected he was, then he was incredibly successful. "As in Fishbone Enterprises?" she asked.

"Yes. I manufacture completed houses for birds, including feeders for them. The build-it-yourself kits are sold mainly through craft stores like Hobby Lobby and Michael's."

It was hard to imagine Jake manufacturing his own line of bird products. But his success explained his nonchalant attitude about buying Kenneth's old house as a getaway place. In Holly's experience, truly successful people didn't brag, they simply moved through life with confidence and purpose the way Jake did.

She could barely take it all in. "How in the world did you get started?"

"My parents are bird-watchers."

"That's interesting," Holly said, surprised again. "You don't strike me as a bird-watcher."

"My parents schedule vacations around the migrations of certain birds," he said, pleased her interest in him was genuine. "It's a hobby that takes them all over the world."

"But you don't study birds?"

"Only the ones in my own backyard. About the age of nine or ten, I became interested in the way birds build their homes and what they eat. One winter I came across some dead ones. My mother explained to me that birds sometimes die from cold and lack of food."

"Is that when you started making houses for them?"

"Yes," Jake said. "Mom let me do my thing in the backyard as long as I bought my own supplies. Dad bought me a workbench and some basic tools and let me have a corner of the garage to build whatever I wanted. I eventually began mixing food."

"You're kidding?"

"It started out with me giving jars of bird food to teachers and relatives at Christmas. I started getting orders for more."

"Where do you sell your bird food?"

"Feed and farm supply companies. I've been rethinking my business, deciding where I wanna take it next."

"What do you think you'll do?"

"I'm not sure," Jake admitted. "I've always delivered quality products, but now the company is becoming too diverse. The food business and the housing business are very different and very profitable. I need to figure out where I want to be in five years, and in ten."

Holly understood the importance of market trends. "Are you thinking of opening a business here maybe?"

"It's a good possibility."

"Who's running your company while you take time off?"

"My parents. Mom keeps the books. Dad manages inventory, shipping and receiving. I also have an excellent support staff. My parents have been a part of the business from the very beginning, first as financial backers, later as advisers and employees. They say they're semiretired, because they get to help their son, stay on top of their hobby, and travel extensively. It's why I can take time off without worrying the company will fall apart without me. I'm lucky."

"Your parents sound terrific, Jake."

"I hope you can meet them."

Holly felt a tingle of awareness. She rarely met parents so early in the dating game. "Come on, I'll show you the rest of the house."

They wound up drinking Vanilla Cokes over ice in the living room. The air was still. No music played in the background, no candles for ambience. There was only cool clean air and conversation.

"Tell me something, Holly."

"What?" she asked, her eyes on his lips.

"How far are you willing to go with this relationship?"

"As far as it works."

Jake needed to confess the truth to Holly, but he was too selfish to do the right thing tonight.

Her name became a sigh on his lips, as he pressed his body over the length of hers on the sofa. For the moment, he held all the power. She was afraid, yes, but of giving too much of herself too soon. Daisy had been right when she'd accused her of choosing easygoing men for convenience. They were easier to control.

Jake wasn't the kind of man she could love for one night, then leave in the morning. Her own feelings were too intense for a brief fling, and he'd told her up front that he wouldn't be staying long. She wanted to be with him, bare and willing right where they lay, but not like this, never like this.

"Wait," she said.

"No."

He kissed her again and she wrapped herself around him, even as he wrapped his will around her. His lovemaking stopped her from thinking, as he crushed her desire to move away, to regroup, to breathe. This wasn't like her. It wasn't, it wasn't. Yet she thrilled to his show of aggression, his man's way of dispensing with words, of relying on action to state his purpose.

Holly let go of her inhibitions. It felt wonderful to be in Jake's arms. Sparkles from her lipstick were scattered over his face and throat as he deepened their kisses. He was strong, strong and hard, and she wanted him.

At last, Jake drew a breath. It was ragged in the cool, still air of her living room, its silence a presence between them. He had more finesse than he'd shown her, more courtesy and control. She deserved better. They both did.

"Right place," he said, "right woman, wrong time."

As Holly watched him collect himself, she realized Jake was no knight in shining armor. This was an angry man, angry in a way that was selfish and deep, selfish because he wouldn't speak of it, deep because it drove him to push a woman he hardly knew into a dangerous mix of sex and sentiment.

In his passion, Jake had revealed his fury to Holly, and the force of his fury had scared her. She didn't know where the rage in him came from, or what was driving it. But it was there, barely controlled and alive.

What had she gotten herself into?

"Jake?" Holly asked in as firm a voice she could muster. "Maybe it's time for you to leave now."

"I'll go," he said. "But I want to see you again."

Four

Daisy caught Holly tidying up bolts of lace when she strolled into her friend's shop for a bit of chitchat. It was a Thursday afternoon, almost closing time, and there were no other customers to interrupt them.

"How's it going with Jake?" Daisy asked.

Holly was almost ashamed to come clean about her mixed feelings, but she'd never been one to keep secrets from someone she trusted. Maybe talking things over with Daisy would help her make up her mind.

"It's going hot and cold," she admitted.

Every ounce the snoop when it came to the lives of her best friends, Daisy settled her bottom onto one chair and propped her feet on another. Her eyes sparkled with the anticipation of a juicy story in the works. Juicy stories made the day that much sweeter.

"Give it up, girl," she coaxed. "Tell me what's happening."

"There's something dark and secretive about him," Holly explained, as she sat down, her feet propped on the same chair Daisy used for her feet. "I don't know what I feel exactly, which is what I mean about the hot and cold."

Daisy was surprised, her face scrunched into a you're-kidding-me expression. This wasn't at all the kind of chitchat she'd been expecting to hear about two of her favorite people. She didn't want to think that her matchmaking abilities were a total washout, but if they were mad, that would explain why she hadn't heard from either Jake or Holly.

"We're talking about Jacob Fishbone, my cousin, right?"

"Right."

"What's wrong? I mean, what happened?"

Absently, Holly folded and refolded a piece of French lace between fingers she couldn't keep still. Nothing was still, not her mind, not her nerves, not her sense that life would ever be the same now that Jake Fishbone had entered into it.

"He's got this wonderful smile, great body—"

"So what's the problem?" Daisy asked, cutting her off.

"What I'm saying, Daisy, is that Jake's, well, he's very intense, you know, private. What you see isn't exactly what you get."

"What, the man's supposed to be an open book or something?"

"You know me, Daze. I'm normally attracted to guys as gabby as I am."

"True."

"Jake has interesting stuff to say, and he's real attentive, but, well, he seems a little mysterious, too. If we talked for hours, I still wouldn't know as much about him as he'd know about me."

Daisy waived a dismissive hand in the air. This was an easy obstacle to get around.

"The guys you like to date are muscle-bound weight-room fanatics, Holly. It's no wonder you feel weird about Jake."

"You've got some nerve."

"Trust me on this, okay, Holly? It's all right for a man to be serious-minded and macho at that same time. There's nothing dark and secretive about it. I married a guy like that and we're doing just fine."

"Give me a break, will you?"

"Okay, like how?"

Holly grimaced. Here was a woman who considered herself an expert on both men under discussion.

"I thought that for a minute," she said. "But I was wrong. Kenneth Gunn and Jake Fishbone are two totally different animals. You strung Kenneth out so long before you agreed to marry him that even I got mad at you. He gave up a lot to be with you. He's patient and considerate, nothing dark about him. We're talking apples and oranges here."

"Okay, what's really bugging you?"

"I think he's got a secret so bad you're waiting for him to tell me first."

"Let's say you're right," Daisy said.

"I'd say you should come clean while we're still friends."

"I love and trust Jake and I know he'd never hurt you or anyone else."

"Hurt? What do you mean hurt?"

"Jake's business is Jake's business."

"Damn it, Daisy, this ain't fair."

Undeterred by Holly's growing anger, Daisy chugged right along, certain that her instincts about Holly and Jake making the perfect couple were right. She subscribed to the notion that time flew too fast to waste it wondering, What if?

"Holly, what good is being friends if we can't tell each other like it really is? Let's be for real, okay? Jake's story is his story to tell. I'd do the same for you."

Swinging her feet to the floor, Holly jumped off her seat, stalked off two steps, turned around, and spoke in a don't-start-tripping tone. "I can't believe you're saying all this. You're supposed to have my back."

"I didn't come here to fight."

"Well, whose side are you on? And don't tell me blood is thicker than water. We're too close and know too much about each other for you to ever go there. If anything, you ought to be neutral."

Daisy didn't shift a muscle, she simply met her friend's belligerent stare in her usual matter-of-fact way. She and Holly went too far back to pretend one didn't know what the other was talking about. As far as she was concerned, family and friends owed it to each other to be more substance than fluff when it came to solving problems.

"You know darn well I can't be a matchmaker and be neutral at the same time. You tend to go for guys with more body than brains, Holly. Jake has both."

"So, now I'm shallow? Gee, thanks."

"Be a woman, why don't you?"

"Be a—"

"Yeah, that's what I said. Admit it, Holly. You're shallow when it comes to a good-looking man in a tight pair of jeans."

"Well," Holly said after twenty long seconds, "relationships with uncomplicated men keep life simple for me. I've never really been attracted to the brooding type of guy like the one in *Wuthering Heights*. You know, the dark loner?"

Daisy raised both her brows, as if to say Holly wasn't making sense.

"*Wuthering Heights?*"

Holly struggled to get her point across to her skeptical friend.

"Some women might think the dark, brooding type of guy is actually sensitive, sensitive meaning tender, if only a woman could get past the brooding part, which is her challenge. I don't like it when men have hidden agendas. I just don't."

"Hidden agendas?" Daisy said.

"The only challenge I want when it comes to a man is what to wear when he takes me out to dinner."

Daisy didn't allow herself to be swayed from her topic. She doubted they'd take this direction in conversation again any time soon, if ever. She went for the full monty. She might not get another chance like this to meddle as far as she dared.

"And you see Jake as dark, dangerous, and full of secrets?"

"Yes, I do, Daisy. I've got reservations about digging around in Jake's dirt to find his gold. I like him. I don't love him."

"I understand, but nobody is talking about love."

"Aren't you?" Holly said in a let's-get-real voice. "I like a movie here and there, a no-strings escort to holiday parties and whatnot, a quick bounce in the bed when the mood strikes. Simple. Simple, Jake ain't."

Daisy crossed her arms and shut her mouth for two minutes. The only sound of significance was a car stereo that shook the storefront windows.

"You went out with Spud Gurber, Holly. I mean, Spud, for Pete's sake. He talks almost as much as you do."

"I know. That's why we had one date, if you can call it that."

Daisy put her feet down, leaned forward, and took

the French lace out of Holly's fingers before it began to fray along the edges.

"I'm not here to talk about Spud," she said. "God love him, girl, but he's a total conversation all by himself."

"No point in disagreeing on that score," Holly said.

"Bottom line is that you're hot about Jake because you like his body, cold because the body you like comes with a brain."

Holly officially closed the shop by turning the signs around. She really was angry. She also didn't want to say anything she'd regret later. She changed the subject.

"How's Kenneth doing? Haven't seen him lately."

Daisy's fat smile was proof Holly's ploy had been a good one. "His carpentry business took an upturn," she said.

"Oh, yeah?"

"He's building a log-cabin-styled fort for a family of boys. A neighbor of that family saw his work and commissioned a playhouse for their daughter, complete with window boxes and a weather vane."

"Word-of-mouth business is often the best advertisement to have," Holly said.

"Amen to that. Seriously though, Holly, what's up with you and Jake?"

"I guess I don't want to fall in love with a man who tells me up front he's only here on a temporary basis."

"Not too temporary."

"The man's on sabbatical, Daze."

"Hey, don't forget Jake bought Kenneth's house. He's got a stake here. Besides all that, nobody's talking about falling in love."

"Get serious. As old as I am, people swear it's way past time for me to tie the knot with somebody and have a few babies. According to people like that, I should always be on the hunt for Mr. Right. According to you, Jake is Mr. Right."

"Well, you are getting long in the tooth," Daisy teased. She had had a similar experience before she met and married her own husband.

"Tell me something, though," Holly said.

"Shoot."

"Why would Jake buy a house for vacation when he could rent one?"

The idea had troubled Holly from the moment she'd made the discovery. Guthrie was totally off the beaten path. It wasn't a place she'd expect a high-profile businessman to choose for himself.

Daisy threw her hands up playfully. "Because he can?" she said.

"I'm not joking."

"Neither am I, Holly. I think you've found a guy you really like, a guy you could easily fall in love with, so you're looking for a way to tear him up."

"That is not true," Holly said, as Daisy's opinion struck a sore nerve.

"Isn't it? Face it, my girl, Jake is a businessman. Businessmen are into investments. Buying a vacation property right across the street from a popular golf course is a definite investment."

"Yeah, I guess so."

"Come off it, will you? If you didn't think a romance with Jake would be exciting, you wouldn't be worrying so much about nothing. Wait, I mean you wouldn't be making up stuff to worry about. Cinnamon or Zenith would love to have a guy like Jake asking them out for dinner or whatever, especially a guy I approve of and love, a guy who happens to be my favorite cousin. You're just being chicken."

"Daisy, Jake doesn't golf, so living in front of a golf course isn't all that big of a wow for him; therefore it can't be that big of a draw for him to move to Guthrie."

"Who says he doesn't golf? Anyway, if he wants to sell his place, the golf course will be a bonus and we both know that, so just stop it, will you? The man builds birdhouses. The man could sit all day on his front porch and stare at birds hanging out in all those trees on his property as well as the ones bordering the golf course for his inspiration."

Holly wasn't convinced. Jake was a troubled man, only Daisy didn't seem to know anything about it, and if she did know, she wasn't giving up the goods. "Golfing and birdhouse building are two very different things."

"Maybe he plans on taking up golfing one day, Holly. Maybe he plans to let his friends vacation at his place when he's gone, people who do golf. Don't forget Guthrie is well known for its festivals and antique shops and what all, as well as for golfing. This is a great little getaway spot for people who need a break from all the wolves in the big bad city. People drive from all over the state just to buy yarn at the shop next door to you—what's that place called again?"

"Sealed with a Kiss."

"Yeah," Daisy said, "and people come from all over the state to buy your lace. This life isn't magic for everybody, but it is magic for those who need to figure out what they wanna do with themselves."

Holly sighed. "All that's true, but—"

"But what?"

"But what man builds birdhouses for a living? I mean, a man his age. I mean, he looks like a boxer or something. He's barely in his thirties."

"Would you feel better if he was retired, a nerd, a mama's boy?" Daisy suggested, heavy on the sarcastic tone.

Holly laughed.

"When you put it that way, I do sound pretty dumb. It's just that I fell in lust at first sight. More than that, though, I could fall for him for real. That alone makes him dangerous, especially when he says up front he's not planning on staying in town long. I don't think an out-of-state romance will work."

"Who knows what can happen, Holly? I wasn't looking for love either when Kenneth came along, but I found it. Go with what you feel."

"I hear you."

Daisy heaved a sigh of relief. She didn't like fighting with her friend, but she wanted two of her favorite people to become favorites of each other. "Thank goodness."

"It seems strange that a guy like him is still single."

Daisy shrugged.

"Maybe the older he gets, the more picky he is, Holly. Like you. I swear, you're really getting to be a stick in the pants."

"You are way, way outta line, Daisy Gunn."

"Very true, but hey."

Holly glared at her, half in jest, half for real. "Yes, Dr. Know It All?"

"Been to his house yet?"

"No."

"Why don't you pay the man a visit?" Daisy suggested.

Holly hadn't heard a peep from Jake since she'd kicked him out of her house. It galled her to think he didn't care enough to follow up. It didn't occur to her to call him.

"Are you suggesting that I show up at the man's house without an invitation?" she asked, appalled, but tempted.

"I certainly am. You're in for a treat."

"I might just do that," Holly said, thinking that after all, this friendship was sanctioned by one of the most decent women she knew.

A woman could tell a great deal about a man by walking through his living space. A surprise visit would let her know if he was a slob or not. If he was, she might find a week's worth of dishes on the counters and laundry scattered around. It might be tough to find a good place to sit. She'd like to see him in his natural habitat.

"Good," Daisy said. "Now, about this lace we've been fooling around with, got any more?"

Five

Speaking with Daisy helped Holly make her mind up about Jake. She wanted to take the romance a step further than a dinner and a half-finished caress among the flowers of her favorite couch in the home that was her refuge against the world.

This involved trusting him personally, something she needed to do in order to get more deeply involved with him. For Holly, trust was about confidence and integrity, assurance that the love given from one to the other was received with care.

Personal trust paved the way to a carnal relationship, the kind that stripped away barriers as naked bodies were revealed, embraced, and absorbed. Being in a trusting, physical relationship with an intense, financially secure man who was single, without children, and totally gorgeous would accelerate her feelings of affection.

Did she have to be in love or think she was in love in order to have sex with Jake? No. But one of her rules for sex with any man was to engage with the type of partner who would make a reliable father.

The man she gave herself to had to be a man she viewed as an asset if she wound up carrying a child that wasn't planned. A love affair was fantasy and romance, but morning sickness and diapers were real. And so was child care.

She'd never discussed this criteria with Daisy or with any of her other girlfriends. Maybe if she had, they wouldn't think she chose men simply for looks and easy disposability once she tired of them. She wasn't that superficial. Sex talks with her parents had stretched beyond basic mechanics into the realm of what-ifs.

What if, her parents had asked, you find yourself with child, only the father refuses accountability? This question had fueled many mother-daughter talks and private musings. Variations of her answer narrowed to one solution for Holly: only share her bed with someone compatible on at least three levels.

Over the years, she'd defined the levels as five, any three of the five scoring an equal point. Holly looked for a guy who didn't walk away from danger, who wasn't afraid to be the first to voice his opinion, who wasn't the last to take action, a man who recognized that no two women were alike, a self-contained man that wasn't looking for a woman to motivate him to excel, but a woman to believe in him as he pursued his dreams.

While there was flexibility in those five levels, there were two criteria for a sex partner that never changed. One: the man had to be mentally tough and physically fit with good form, bones, and teeth. Two: the man had to be social, literate, forward thinking, and drug free.

Her partner didn't need a college degree, a thick bank account, his own property, or a fancy car. He didn't need to be domestic. She didn't care if he had children, as long as he used his time and his money to rear them.

She didn't care if he came from a family of oddballs and misfits, or if he'd been raised near the poverty line. She cared about quality. Quality men desired quality women, which is how she defined herself.

If the fact she had a rating system made her shallow, why then, that didn't bother Holly. She was the kind of woman who played for keeps. Like parenting, marriage for Holly was an ultimate commitment, one she took seriously.

Yes, Jake Fishbone had a secret, a secret Daisy obviously knew about, but since he hit all seven points on her rating scale, Holly felt strong about her decision to open her heart. Unless the man had committed some sin she considered unpardonable, such as rape, molestation, or murder, then she saw no reason to change her mind.

Holly's commitments were set in stone. Stone could be broken, but in order to eliminate it entirely, the stone had to be pulverized into dust, then the dust blown away. The kind of woman who played for keeps was also the kind of woman who gave her all.

She came from a family who believed in taking chances. Taking chances on people was a way to crack the lid of her small town world by allowing fresh ideas inside, new blood, alternative points of view.

Jake Fishbone was an entrepreneur in a business that catered to hobbyists, as her business did. Together, they could discuss the quirks of business ownership, how he made the transition from a regional entity into a national corporation, information that might help her expand as well. Oh, yes, there were pluses.

Did she need to dissect his secrets in order to enjoy him? No. Falling in love was about hope in a future that was deeply meaningful and physically exclusive. Holly wasn't in love, wasn't sure she was falling in love, but she felt she could love Jake, that if she had a child with him he wouldn't run off, that he was a man of integrity.

Contrary to her past behavior, Holly was ready to take a chance on love, even though she had one serious reservation: the rage that Jake worked so hard to conquer, and that Daisy refused to discuss, an attitude in keeping with her bleeding heart reputation. In this regard, Holly's decision to stick with Jake was a leap of faith.

Daisy had once allowed a troubled man into her life. She had welcomed him into her home, exposed him to the tight scrutiny of her intimate circle of friends, had even helped him solve a murder when being involved in murder went against the grain of her pacifist, self-sufficient lifestyle.

Daisy had risked her heart and her credibility with her friends to aid a troubled man, only to be rewarded with the kind of love that lasts a lifetime. In the end, the troubled man, now her husband, made peace with his past and moved on with his life. Perhaps Jake would do the same, make peace, and take a leap of faith of his own.

Feeling revved from her heart-to-heart talk with Daisy, Holly stopped at home to refresh herself before visiting Jake. She wanted to shower, renew her makeup and hair, get her feminine arsenal ready and primed for a night fueled with lovemaking. Based on their chemistry, she didn't think he'd turn her away.

After they made love, she imagined, he'd confess his secrets to her. He'd tell her about the woman she suspected was the trouble in his past, and if he was on the rebound, why then, their romance had a time limit to it, the duration of his sabbatical.

His vacation provided an excuse for them both to

back out, claiming the distance between them was inconvenient, inflexible, or impractical. If her heart was broken when Jake was gone, well, she'd store the memories they made together and go on. Nothing was guaranteed, and if there was happiness to enjoy today, she was determined to have it.

Like she always did when she arrived home, Holly checked her mailbox. Inside the dark green container she purchased from Daisy's garden shop was an envelope. Inside the envelope was a picture.

The instant camera snapshot was taken in black and white. The film appeared recent. It featured a dark-skinned young woman, a woman who looked as if she knew how to have a good time, a woman in her early thirties.

Flicking the picture over in her hand, Holly was disturbed by the handwritten particulars. On the back of the picture, marked in slim red permanent ink, was the chilling message:

> *Rayna Holdenbrook*
> *Murdered*
> *Suspect is Jake Fishbone*
> *Beware*

There was no return address on the envelope, just Holly's name, her mailing address, and a postmark from Blue Springs, Arkansas. Jake was from Blue Springs.

Pivoting quickly, Holly returned to her late-model Amigo, jumped in, tossed her mail and purse on the passenger seat, and threw the snappy SUV in reverse. She was headed to Jake's house all right, but she wasn't looking for a good time.

She was looking for answers. Right now she felt used, angry, manipulated. In her heart, she'd known Jake's secret involved another woman. If the police considered him a murder suspect, his reluctance to come clean made sense. If he was guilty, he might want to separate himself from the crime by moving to Guthrie. Innocence would explain his rage.

It upset her that someone he knew was trying to run a head game on her. Because he'd passed her rating system, and because Daisy had given the relationship her blessing, Holly wanted to give Jake the chance to explain the damning picture.

She pounded on his door hard enough to hurt the pinky side of her right fist. He answered the door in a pair of tight jeans and nothing else, not even a smile. She shoved the picture in his face.

"The postmark on this envelope says Blue Springs, Arkansas," she said. "What's going on, Jake?"

The one minute of silence was heavy.

"What does Daisy say about all this?" he asked.

Holly was taken aback. Not once had she considered calling Daisy, and to think Jake thought of it first shifted her entire perspective. He was surprised to see her, but not so surprised his brains were scrambled. He had the presence of mind to wonder if anyone else knew she'd come alone to see him.

Holly couldn't believe the pickle she'd put herself into. This was not a normal situation. Under normal conditions, she would never do what she was doing right now, which was act first and ask questions later.

"I didn't tell her."

Jake's eyes narrowed, calculatedly. He perused the length of her, his nostrils flaring just the slightest bit. He was mad as hell. But was he mad at the person who'd mailed her the picture, or was he mad at her for confronting him before he'd told her the truth himself?

"You think I've done something wrong, so why come here by yourself?"

Damned if she knew, but his stare said two different things. She couldn't tell if he wanted to shake her or kiss her. For all she knew he had a more sinister thought in mind, such as his hard squeezing hands around her stupid little throat.

Holly froze to the spot.

Now that she was here, she was afraid to ask serious questions about the woman in the photograph. What had Rayna meant to him exactly? Had they been lovers? How was Rayna killed?

Holly had spent more time applying lipstick that morning than she'd spent thinking about what she'd do after she confronted him.

Mesmerized, she watched his gaze travel to the left and right behind her. All was quiet on this normally busy stretch of back road; even the golf course across the street from Jake's house was short of people on the greens.

When he opened his front door a little wider, she noticed his place smelled like chicken fajitas. She loved chicken fajitas, but she loved her neck even more. She needed to get back home, call Daisy, call Zenith, call Cinnamon—no, she didn't want to call Cinnamon Hartfeld, because Cinnamon couldn't keep a secret to save her own life. If she called her parents, they would call the police, and to them the police was Spud Gurber.

Hot damn, she was in a fix. What she needed to do was . . .

"Come inside, Holly. Let's talk like normal people.

I've got some of that D.G.'s coffee Daisy guzzles like water. This is gonna take a while."

He sounded normal, reasonable even. She trusted him, and if the leap of faith was bigger than she thought at first, then she'd deal with it. Certainly there was a reasonable explanation for the anonymous picture. Certainly. She squared her shoulders.

"Were you expecting something like this to happen? Is that why you're always looking at exits and all that, Jake? Why you're so careful? You figured someone would find out where you are and come to mess things up?"

"Yes."

Holly should have called him on the phone. Mostly naked as he was, every muscle above his just-right waist spoke of supreme strength and virility. He could do serious damage with a backhand to her face if he decided to cut loose. He could . . .

"Who was she, Jake?"

"My friend."

"Is it true, then, that she was . . . murdered?"

"Yes, but I didn't kill her."

The half-naked man was reaching for her. His scuffed-up hands were going to wring her silly neck. He was going to haul her off into his secluded retreat and . . . *Oh, hell no*, she thought. *No. No. No.*

She stomped his bare foot.

Jake tried but failed to curb a dozen cuss words. He was fluent. He was incensed. He was not in control of himself. He didn't want to choke her, but he did want to shake her after she stomped his foot and ran away.

"Holly!"

She didn't look back. Looking back is what dummies do in the movies. She wasn't a dummy and this wasn't a movie. This man's body was a long, dark, deadly weapon. He might do more than wring her neck. He might . . .

She jumped in the car, hit the master lock for all the doors, and rammed the key into the ignition.

Jake slammed his palm against the glass of the driver's-side window. His stare was unreadable, but his lips were hard and cruel with anger.

"Holly!"

The man was enormous, grizzly bear size. To hell with being civil. Her rear tires kicked dust from his gravel drive into his face. What did she care if she accidentally ran some or all of him over? He'd chased her, hadn't he? He was going to break her car window, wasn't he? She had the right to protect herself by any means necessary, which is what she planned to do.

Someone from Blue Springs, Arkansas, had sent her a picture of a dead woman, a woman Jake once knew. Someone was trying to scare her. And that someone had succeeded.

She was, at this moment, way beyond plain scared. She was stuck-on-a-broken-down-roller-coaster-at-the-top-of-the-ride scared. What if his feet hadn't been bare, or if she hadn't been a former track star? He'd have caught her, that's what.

She might feel like an idiot later, but as she shot a glance in the rearview mirror, Holly was glad she'd decided to leave as hastily as she'd arrived. Jake was hopping around on one foot in the rocks, his eyes screaming bloody murder.

Six

Kenneth tried to calm a wild-eyed Holly while his coward wife took her time turning off the water sprinklers in the hybrid tea garden. Daisy was finishing her work in the garden center when Holly skidded her Amigo to a stop in the driveway.

It was a long skid, in which the Gunns were left speechless. In her haste, Holly hit a huge stack of ready-to-go bags of pine bark mulch with the much-used front bumper of her car. The busted bags would be taped up and on sale tomorrow.

Tomorrow.

Somehow they had to get through the rest of the day, hostile friendships and meddling relatives intact.

Somehow.

When the bags busted, Daisy simply panicked. Eyes wide, brows raised, her mouth sprung open, she looked at Kenneth, who, based on his deep and personal experience with her, understood she wanted him to referee.

Because he loved his wife, Kenneth braced himself for the upcoming battle of tears as he turned his gaze from his wife to his wife's friend. Holly was drama with a capital D as she flounced her way across the gravel drive in a floral print that matched the landscape.

If the situation wasn't so serious—and Kenneth knew it was serious because he knew why Jake had moved to Guthrie—he might have laughed at the ruined bags and the reckless Holly, but he couldn't.

Jake was in the kind of trouble Holly should have been warned about in advance. Because he loved his wife, Kenneth had gone along with her request to wait for Jake to tell Holly about his past whenever he felt the time was right.

Since Fishbone had come to town, there had been nothing but surprises. It had surprised Kenneth that his wife's matchmaking had actually resulted in a first date. Now that Jake's secret was obviously out, hell had a name and that name was Holly.

Kenneth had never seen her this angry, had never seen her eyes blurred by tears she dashed away one after the other. He hated to see her cry today. It was probably a good thing his wife was giving her old friend a few minutes to pull herself together.

He bet Daisy wished now that she'd listened to him when he'd warned her that all her good intentions might backfire, which they apparently had. Jake had played with fire by not telling Holly the truth.

They had all played with fire.

While she waited for Daisy, Holly couldn't sit still. She paced the kitchen, barely listening to Kenneth's suggestion she use plain common sense to assess her problem, which in turn added to her agitation.

She was in a jam, couldn't anybody understand that simple, crazy fact? And why did her heart hurt so bad?

"Bottom line, Holly," he said after he listened to her talk with hardly a breath for air, "is that I trust him."

Jam and all, Holly felt a huge sense of relief. As a former private detective, Kenneth had dealt with a number of men who were true criminals. She felt she could trust his instincts on this particular subject.

"That carries a lot of weight with me, it really does," she admitted, as she forced herself to stop wringing her hands. "I guess I went to see him for an explanation about the picture; then when I got there, I lost my nerve."

"Why?"

Talking to Kenneth was therapeutic for Holly, who suspected Daisy was taking her time in the garden so he could calm her down. Besides that reason, Daisy also didn't want to answer questions about her cousin's character, or fight with her longtime friend.

Holly didn't blame Daisy for procrastinating. She'd probably pull the same move if their situations were reversed. There was a future at stake, their future as best friends.

Holly propped a hip against the kitchen counter, at home in the gentle clutter that surrounded her. There were mugs in the double sink, two forks, and two dessert plates, remnants from the Gunns' afternoon break together.

"I started wondering if Jake had harmed that Rayna Holdenbrook," she admitted quietly after a superlong sigh that helped her shoulders relax.

To her own secret self, Holly also admitted she'd been rattled by Jake's half-naked appearance at his front door. Sexy, smart, dangerous, Jake Fishbone was a beefed-up bobcat in his recently purchased neck of the Guthrie woods. Tight muscles. Hard body. Agile. Quick. Easily mistaken for a half-wild tomcat.

Up close there'd been a feral element to him, suppressed violence he kept hidden under perfect manners, excellent speech, and top drawer success.

Holly wasn't fooled any longer by his masquerade: she'd seen his power. She'd been right to be afraid. She was afraid because slowly, inescapably, he was ruining her taste for other men.

Sprawled in a chair, Kenneth was a warrior in the wings if it came down to it, but first, he wanted an orderly report of what happened. He knew all the players involved, but something didn't jibe. "You think the picture was a message of warning about Jake?" he asked.

"Yes."

Kenneth folded his arms across his chest, his light brown eyes cool as they stared at his surprise guest from a face that looked like carved ebony. There was definitely something Holly wasn't telling him. "But why would you be suspicious of him in the first place?"

Holly hedged. Leave it to Kenneth to ferret out the slimmest niggle of doubt. She supposed it made sense that he didn't take her words at face value, seeing as he had been a private detective before he married Daisy.

"You mean before I got the picture, was I suspicious of him?"

Kenneth was patient. Now that he had a prime seat in the Daisy-Holly-Jake soap opera, he relished his ability to participate. Maybe his expertise would come in handy.

"Were you?"

"Kind of," she confessed.

"Why?"

She told him the same reasons she'd once shared with Daisy. To her own ears, she sounded lame.

"Maybe my wife is right," Kenneth said, as he removed his carpentry belt from the waist of his paint-stained work jeans, then set it on the table.

"Maybe you did think Jake was too good to be true, and ran scared because of it."

Holly was ashamed of herself, ashamed and embarrassed. She'd caused a scene at Jake's, a scene at Daisy's, all because she was running off raw emotion. She sat in a chair with a thump and a hard sigh.

"Man, that sounds stupid."

Kenneth didn't agree. "You've got to make up your mind if he's a good guy or a bad one, Holly, then take it from there."

"I should have heard him out instead of running him over."

"You sure as hell should have," said a voice from the direction of the living room.

It was Jake.

He wore a long-sleeved shirt that wasn't buttoned, and sandals he hadn't bothered to strap to his feet. He stared at her as if she were the only person in the room, and she might as well have been, because she forgot all about their audience.

Kenneth was content to keep his mouth shut. The less he said, the more he'd learn.

Holly hopped from her chair so fast, she almost lost her balance, her heart pumping madly. Jake was here. What must he think? What must he see? Was her hair standing all over her head because she'd raked her fingers through it fourteen times in ten minutes?

His voice was low and ominous.

"Anybody ever tell you, Holly, you can't drive worth a damn?"

It was clear to them all she'd been too flustered to realize he'd followed her. It was also clear he'd been outside talking to Daisy. If she'd checked her rearview mirror at least once, she'd have seen him behind her.

Guthrie didn't have so many cars on the road, especially the back roads, for her not to figure out somebody was hot on her trail. She should have noticed something, or at least she should have considered the possibility that he might chase after her.

She'd make a lousy detective.

"You're limping," she said.

"My foot was under the tire when I banged on your window. You also stomped on the same foot before you made your escape."

"Uh," she said, "I'm sorry."

He continued to have eyes only for her. He wanted her, more now than he had when she kicked him out of her house. Still, she had to come to him because she wanted to be with him. It was the only way their relationship would work.

"You were right to take off. I was angry."

Holly figured they were lucky Spud Gurber hadn't been driving by their little altercation. Had Spud or even one of his fellow police officer friends spotted them fighting, Jake would probably be at the police station answering serious questions about more than the picture of a dead woman.

They'd want to know who he was, exactly. What was he doing in Guthrie, exactly? Did he think he could fight with Holly and not be punished? Spud's friends knew her. They didn't know Jake.

"Make up your mind," he said, more aware of her mental struggle than she gave him credit for. "We're either on or we're off. I don't do the back-and-forth thing."

Wearing her standard gardening gear, green rubber clogs, jeans, and plain cotton shirt, Daisy stood beside her husband. At one hundred twenty pounds, she was a tiny dynamo beside his two-hundred-pound, six-foot-plus frame.

"Why don't you two go outside and talk?" she suggested. "We'll be here if either of you wants us."

When neither Jake nor Holly bothered to move, Kenneth added his weight to his wife's suggestion.

"What you both need is information," he said. "Holly needs to hear the truth from you, Jake. You need to know how she's gonna handle the truth. Me and Daisy will be in the kitchen if you need us."

Settled in chairs on the front porch, Holly said, "What happened to the girl in the picture, Jake?"

"She was murdered."

His secret was worse than she expected. She could hardly get the idea stuffed into her mind, but she tried.

"Were you a suspect?"

"Still am."

The truth was brutal, but Holly took it like a champ. She'd asked for this, all of it, but she was glad she wasn't alone, that her friends were nearby. "How did she die, Jake?"

"Multiple stab wounds. The police are convinced Rayna knew her killer."

Holly scrunched her shoulders and body up, as if to ward off physical blows. If she'd known all this in advance, she'd never have kissed Jake Fishbone. They had almost made love. What if they'd gone all the way? What if . . .

"Does Daisy know about all this, Jake?"

"Yes."

Holly felt betrayed, stabbed in the chest herself. There were tears in her eyes, angry, bitter tears, but they would not fall. "She should have told me."

"Daisy didn't set out to hurt or scare you any more

than I did. My motive for coming to Guthrie was to re-group, to get my head on straight again. That hasn't changed."

"You couldn't do that in Blue Springs? Regroup, I mean?"

"No."

"Why?"

"I saw Rayna everywhere, walking into our favorite restaurant, driving past me in her car, but when I looked twice, I knew I was looking at someone else." Jake ran a hand over his face, distorting his features in the process. "Since her death, I've been obsessed with finding her killer and killing him myself. Meeting you wasn't part of the plan."

Holly reached out to him, putting her fingers around his wrist, as if to anchor him in the present. His rage over Rayna's murder was a tangible force between them. It was a rage that had never been directed at her, a woman he had only touched with kindness. This man was Daisy's blood kin, and Kenneth trusted him, and despite his problems, Holly wanted to trust him, too.

For a woman who relished a good gossip, Holly wasn't sure what to say during this pivotal crisis. From the start, she'd known any relationship with Jake would be filled with unlimited possibilities. She never imagined those possibilities included malice, murder, and betrayal.

She'd looked forward to the challenge of him, of getting to know a man who reminded her of Daisy's husband. Kenneth was, even now, levelheaded, ob-servant, intelligent, as was Jake. Yes, there were possibilities, but in the mix was the unpardonable sin of murder.

Rayna Holdenbrook's murder remained unsolved, the man suspected of killing her the man Holly had decided she wanted to be involved with, secrets and all. He'd admitted he rarely kidded around, and she didn't blame him. He had little to kid about.

With his anger unleashed, Jake truly did look like a gunslinger. His rugged face didn't ask for either forgiveness or understanding. His movements remained confident, his attitude one of command that stimulated the rebel inside her soul. She'd never been shy and this was no time to be subtle.

"Were you in love?" she asked.

"We were in love with our careers. Both professions involved extensive entertaining and networking. Travel. We served as each other's escorts. It was a comfortable arrangement, and we were happy to keep things the way they were."

"But, why are you still a suspect?"

"Her killer hasn't been caught. I'm as likely a candidate as anyone else in her life. I'm still a suspect because the police weren't able to establish a reason for me to kill her. They don't see how I benefit."

Holly understood now, about the bitterness behind his eyes. She also understood why Daisy and Kenneth had wanted to give him a chance to get his life on track.

"What do you think the picture is all about?"

His answer came quick, his voice as rough as his face was hard. "Someone wants to sabotage my credibility."

"With me, you think?"

"You, the town in general, who knows? At this point, the why isn't as important as the who. I want to know who's got it in for me, so I can face him down."

"Let me help."

"Less than an hour ago, you tried to run me over, Holly."

She wasn't offended by his skeptical tone. He had reason to doubt her decision. She'd doubt it too, if she were him. "Ever been in a spot where you didn't know how much you enjoyed a privilege until the honor was taken away?"

"Yeah."

"The relationship growing between us is a privilege, and I almost lost it because I felt insecure. I'm used to doing my own things my own way, and so, I think, are you."

He nodded his head, slowly.

"Rayna's death showed me how shallow I was to settle for escort status in a beautiful woman's life. When I left Blue Springs, I vowed to live every day as if it's my last one. I like you, Holly. I want you because I like you. It's as simple as that for me."

He offered his hand, in both a show of strength and of vulnerability. She took the hand he offered and smiled.

"Hi," she said. "My name is Holly Hunter. I own a lace shop in town, but to tell you the truth, my work is hardly work at all, because I enjoy it so much. Basically, I'm a career girl faced with a guy who's got serious problems that make me nervous. In spite of all that, I'd like to help."

He squeezed her hand.

"My name is Jake Fishbone. I'm CEO of a national corporation, but all I can think about is solving the murder of my close friend. The last thing I need is another close relationship with a woman, but here I am. I accept your offer to help."

"Good," she said. "Now, let's get some of that coffee

Daisy's brewing. I can't think of better people to brainstorm with than the Gunns."

The two couples wound up sitting in the combined living and dining room, a unique setting dominated by red sofas, green tables, and purple lamps. Although Daisy was a professional gardener by trade, there wasn't a plant in sight.

Daisy spoke first.

"I got you two together because of your availability and your compatibility. I know each of you very well, and so it concerns me that fear is a factor in your dealings with each other."

"Frankly," Kenneth said, "it surprises me, too."

"So," Daisy said, "I wonder if, rather than fear, what Holly really felt initially was some sort of premonition of danger."

Kenneth was shaking his head before his wife could finish.

"I don't believe in getting weird and spooky," he said, "but Daisy might be on to something with her premonition angle. After all, there has been a murder, which remains unsolved."

"Yes," Jake said, "and I'm still a suspect because the police can't rule me out."

Kenneth looked at Jake. He had honored his friend's wish for privacy, and had kept their relationship as relaxed as possible. He understood about the need for fresh beginnings, that sometimes honest men were accused wrongly of capital crimes.

"Do you have a case file?" the former private detective asked, aware that by doing so he was no longer neutral. This question changed the scope of their relationship by placing a strain on their friendship. The detective was back in action.

"I built one of my own," Jake said, "news clippings mostly, and copies of any legal documents I could get my hands on."

"Good," Kenneth said, "I'd like to see what you've got."

Jake's gaze swept each person briefly, lingering on Holly the longest. He had deluded himself into thinking he could take a mental break from the drama that was his everyday life, but the truth could not wait.

"Rayna is everywhere," he said, "everywhere."

"Sometimes the past doesn't let us start over," Daisy said. "Maybe whoever sent the picture to Holly doesn't want you to forget."

"Maybe."

Kenneth leaned forward.

"Tell us what you know so far, Jake."

"My own search for Rayna's killer hasn't been random, because I knew her intimately. Based on physical evidence discovered by the police, whoever killed her also knew her. I must know who did it, but for the life of me, I can't think of anyone I find even remotely suspicious. I can't think of anyone crazy enough to commit murder."

"You're saying there was no sign of forced entry or struggle," Kenneth said.

"None, but the police seem to think her death might not have been premeditated, that she might have been killed during a fit of anger."

Holly wrapped her arms around herself.

"A crime of passion."

"Yes," Jake said. "Looking at it from that angle, I tried to think of who she was emotionally attached to, and vice versa."

"Go on," Kenneth said.

"Her business partner is married, but rumor has it, Dirk Adams was prone to extramarital affairs. It's possible he and Rayna were involved, and when she tried to break it off, he became angry enough to kill her."

Kenneth listened intently. It amazed him that Jake hadn't confided in him before now. The stress of his problems was a terrible burden, especially for an innocent man.

"Her partner would have motive and opportunity, but something tells me you don't think he committed the crime."

"I don't. They had a business to run together, so it wasn't practical for Dirk to bring suspicion on himself that way. The business would suffer, which it has, because Rayna was the people-person part of their venture. She dealt with the public, he ran the nuts and bolts behind the scenes. Besides, I've seen them together enough to find it hard to believe they were carrying on an affair that was so volatile, he would kill her. They just got along exceptionally well."

"But, the police consider him a suspect?" Kenneth asked.

"Yes, like me, there was no clear benefit from her death. His wife knew of his relationships with other women and she didn't seem to care as long as he maintained her expensive habits. Marlene Adams is a clotheshorse. She never drives a car more than two years straight. She hires someone to cook and clean. She doesn't want children."

"You didn't like her," Daisy said.

"No, I didn't, but she wasn't my problem. I heard about her escapades now and then from Rayna."

"Who else is significant?" Kenneth asked.

"I don't know. The police investigated the men she

came into contact with through her job. They contacted the maintenance people in her building, clients, and so on. Nothing. Dirk and I are the recurrent theme when it comes to the men in her life."

"But," Holly said, satisfied until now to watch, listen, and learn, "who says Rayna's killer is a man?"

Seven

Holly followed Jake back to his place as a show of commitment. Her entering his home, knowing he was suspected of murder, spoke more deeply to him than any words she might express.

He dressed his home simply, with a lived-in clutter in keeping with his personality. His furnishings were big and functional, decoration minimal, the atmosphere warm and friendly. There were no weapons of destruction lying about on the tabletops, no walls covered with images of Rayna Holdenbrook to highlight his obsession.

If anything, the normal state of Jake's home was proof he'd been telling the truth about why he'd come to Guthrie. He really had tried to create order and sanctuary away from Blue Springs. To Holly, it felt as if days had passed instead of hours since she ran over his foot.

As he turned on lights inside his home, she realized that instinctively she'd known he wasn't a true danger to her, just as he had realized that she was the remedy he needed to get his life back on track. Since brainstorming with the Gunns, he'd been able to let his guard down, as Holly had hoped he would.

"I'm glad you're here," he said.

She watched as wonder softened his face.

"Truth is, Jake, I want to nail the guy who's trying to nail you."

Now that she'd committed to his cause, her eyes were those of a crusader. She wasn't a woman who indulged in halfhearted endeavors. She was able to grasp and assimilate information, to decide what was important to do now versus what could wait for later. The truth could not wait.

Jake shared her thoughts. "I'll show you my case file."

They moved into the kitchen, where they sat at the table. It was an inexpensive glass top with a rattan base and four matching chairs. There were paper napkins in a wooden holder, a set of rooster salt and pepper shakers beside it.

Holly settled into her decision to be with him. Their being together felt constructive and worthwhile. Maybe they were on the right path to justice for Rayna, to healing for Jake. It was a turning point.

"The world begins and ends in the kitchen," she said, as she took in the bachelor pad surroundings.

"What do you mean?"

"The living room is often comfortable, but the kitchen has everything. There's the usual table that makes a large, wide work surface. The light is bright. Food and drinks are handy. There's usually a window with a view of either the front or backyard."

"True."

"It's easy to take it all for granted."

"Yeah," Jake said, thinking how easily he could be in the Blue Springs jail.

Holly was the first woman he'd entertained in his new home who wasn't a relative. His Guthrie relatives had closed ranks around him by helping to keep his true identity a secret. Like Daisy, his extended family was protective of him. Holly looked lovely, even though her makeup had disappeared after she'd hugged and cried with Daisy as they'd shored up their friendship before parting.

"Want coffee or anything else to drink?" he asked.

"Coke if you've got it."

"I do."

"Good. I like it over ice."

"No problem."

He pulled classic white paper napkins from the holder on the table, and set the glasses on top of them. From the cupboard, he grabbed a clear dinner plate. He spread Pepperidge Farms Chessmen cookies on top.

Jake didn't strike Holly as the domestic type, but she supposed that because he lived alone, he'd acquired a rough set of survival skills when it came to being a host. Still, there was humor in the moment.

"Cookies?" she said, as she raised a brow in jest.

It was only packaged shortbread cookies he served, nothing fancy, just tasteful. But being served by six feet of gray-eyed chocolate man put a fresh spin on dining at home, especially when home was his place.

Jake took note of the irony in her eyes.

"I like to munch while I work," he explained, then made a toast to her with his full glass of iced Coke.

He felt lucky, her presence a victory. She didn't treat him like a monster, as others had done in Blue Springs. It surprised him how quickly people had chosen to distance themselves from him once they heard he was suspected of murder.

"Me too."

Jake removed the swollen case file from a kitchen

drawer. He kept it beneath two neat stacks of dish towels, all of them white and checkered with green.

Her eyes widened in disbelief.

"I can't believe you'd treat something this important so casually. I mean, anybody could grab your stuff that way."

"Would you think of looking for this file in the kitchen?"

"No."

"I didn't think so."

She thumbed back a lock of stray hair, unaware the simple gesture disturbed Jake by reminding him of Rayna, who often toyed with her hair. Long and brown, Rayna's hair had been streaked with gold. He liked Holly's short, bouncing style.

"I spend a lot of time in this room," he said. "It's a convenient place to spread out. I've turned one of the bedrooms into an office, but I like it here best."

Holly sipped her Coke in silence. She wasn't fooled by the cookies. He was concerned she would bolt. That manila envelope held details of a major crime, and a suspect in the murder was giving her one last chance to part ways.

He rested his back against his chair, not touching her, but wanting to touch her. He'd built his business on discipline and perseverance. Romance wasn't business, but like the best business relationships, it was constructed on solid ground.

Her trust was vital, the reason he waited her out.

After a time she said, "I'm ready."

When Jake opened the file, Holly wanted to throw up. He left the file open, the contents of which were the demon he'd been fighting. She needed to see it in order to believe it. The crime was real, and so was his motivation to solve it.

Having her believe in him added to Jake's energy pool. Eventually, Holly squared her mind, lifted her chin. It wasn't easy to master her fear, but she did.

"How did you get access to such . . . detail? I mean, some of these photos are so, uh, graphic."

"There's a way to get just about anything."

She tried to suppress a shudder and failed. Her head swam. Her palms sweated. This was for real, and now they were in the thick of it together. Even if she left, she wouldn't be able to forget what she'd just seen. He'd known this. He'd given her the space she needed to walk away from him, repelled by her discoveries.

She'd been on a roller coaster of emotion. He'd been on the roller coaster with her, and had known she'd be sick at the end of the ride, no matter what he said or did to prepare her, and yet she had stayed.

She respected the courage it took for Jake to stay on point with his quest when nearly everyone was against him. It was so much easier to let the police and their crime specialists handle the problem, to say there was nothing he could do because he wasn't qualified. Jake took his friendships seriously, and so did she.

"This is all ground zero for me, Jake."

"What's the first thing you notice about the case?" he asked, as he watched the subtle moves of the muscles in her face.

The fine flickers of movement gave her the look of vibrancy he enjoyed so much. Despite the dramatic moments of the day, she believed that good would triumph over evil; otherwise she wouldn't share this simple meal with him in his home.

"Well," she said, "I've noticed that you call this . . . matter a case and not a situation or even a problem."

His shrug was eloquent.

"I guess it's a sign of the times," he said. "It's hard not to read a crime novel or watch a crime show and not be influenced by clichés or trite terminology."

"Case file it is, then."

Holly read its contents for a few minutes, sifting through the typed reports, the handwritten notes, the photographs, and the newspaper clippings. She looked up to find him watching her. She couldn't hide her alarm, her revulsion, her respect that he'd held this horror in his mind all alone.

"I can't believe you're still here, Holly."

His eyes held wonder, of her, and of the evening neither was in a hurry to rush. She wasn't running, wasn't turning her face away from him with second thoughts, when there were several reasons why she still should.

Instead, she touched his right forearm with her fingers. She couldn't imagine him using that same arm to wield a deadly weapon against a woman in cold blood, especially a woman he cared deeply about. And yet, someone had done that very thing.

Rayna Holdenbrook was a specter in the room with them, a restless spirit caught between the living and the dead. She might have been a flesh-and-blood woman for all the commotion she caused. She was a turbulence in the atmosphere, her spirit in motion in this room.

"I'm sorry this happened to you, Jake. It's a horrible mess. Clearly, based on the time frame of the murder, you have no alibi."

"No."

Holly closed the ugly case file.

Matching his mood, she measured her breath, as if by moving slowly, by thinking carefully, the vital clue they sought would reveal itself. Once revealed, the past would lose its ability to hurt them. In this regard, hope was power.

Despite all the negative, damning, circumstantial evidence, Holly had faith that in the end, all would be well. Faith was about believing in the improbable. In this instance, the improbable would be a confession from the killer.

"This is all so bizarre, Jake. I feel wiped out from all the stuff that's gone on in the last couple of hours."

"I went through the same process," he admitted. "Shock. Fear. Anger. The need for revenge is what keeps me going."

The case file was returned to its drawer, but its presence had spoiled the comfort of the kitchen. They resettled into the living room.

"Tell me about her," Holly said.

"We were friends."

Such grief, Holly noticed, in those three words. She considered what she'd learned about Jake so far. He was considerate, evidenced by his attitude with Daisy, a meddling woman with good intentions toward him.

He didn't talk too much, but he seemed to notice everything that went on around him, evidenced by the way his eyes surveyed a room. He catalogued contents without commenting on them or touching them, storing them in memory. But somehow, he had missed the clue that Rayna's life was in danger.

"So," Holly said, "you feel guilty you weren't able to stop what happened to her. Is that what's driving your need for revenge?"

He closed his eyes. Using his thumb and index finger, he massaged the bridge of his nose. "I should have seen something, heard . . . something."

"Had she been under pressure before she died?" Holly asked.

"She said she was having second thoughts about her career. We never got into the why of it. I hadn't thought she was serious, because she enjoyed her work."

"People change," Holly said. "Maybe she wanted to move on."

"I had considered talking to Dirk about it, but we haven't spoken since the funeral."

Holly took a moment to digest this bit of news. "If Rayna wanted to break off the business partnership and start her own, say by stealing corporate marketing and sales strategy as well as key clientele, wouldn't you think that would be a motive for murder?"

"Yes."

"Do you think he did it," Holly asked, "killed her, I mean?"

"No."

"Why not?"

"He loved her the way good friends do. The way I did. Besides that, he needed her for the business. If she wanted out, really wanted out, I doubt he would have stopped her."

"Does he think you killed her?"

"I don't think so."

"Why not," Holly asked, "when the police can't rule you out?"

"My relationship with Rayna was independent of the relationship Dirk had with her. He knows the truth about Rayna and myself, that I wouldn't hurt her."

"Based on what's in this file, I think the reason you aren't in jail now is that the police couldn't place you with the body at the time of death. Did you take a lie detector test?"

"Yes, and I passed."

Holly tried to imagine Jake in prison garb. She couldn't. There had to be a solution to this mess. She just hoped it was somewhere close and that it came sometime soon. "What we need is a list of your enemies, and hers."

"That's where I draw a blank," Jake said, as he rolled his shoulders.

Holly dug a pen from her purse. It took her a while to find one because her everyday handbag was more like a suitcase. Her chiropractor warned her repeatedly to downsize, advice she ignored. She almost always had what she needed in her purse.

"I'm not in a hurry, Jake. I've got all night."

His eyes devoured her, but he kept his mouth shut. Right woman. Right place. Wrong time. "So do I."

Holly kicked off her shoes to get comfortable while they started on the list together. They began with the victim's brother. He'd told Jake at the funeral that he'd kill him if he found out he was guilty.

"Are you sure you can take Rayna's brother seriously?" Holly asked.

"All death threats are serious."

"Yeah, but I mean her entire family must have it in for you. It's got to be hard to narrow her family down to one man."

"Another reason why I left Blue Springs."

Holly doodled with the pen for a while. "What about Rayna? What about an ex-boyfriend or something like that?"

"Rayna's relationships with men were rocky. Our

arrangement worked because it was based on convenience only."

Holly nixed a sigh at the direction the list of enemies was taking. "No wonder the police can't rule anybody out. There aren't many people to choose from and the people they've got don't have decent motives."

"Exactly."

Holly tossed the pen onto the coffee table. It rolled between the *TV Guide* and a magazine on birdwatching.

"Okay," she said. "What if her death was all about your business and screwing it up in order to make you fail somehow? Did any of your competitors know Rayna?"

The set of Jake's hard, bearded jaw was grim. "That would be a stretch. I haven't received threats to the business. I don't think Dirk has either, and he had more to lose than I did. His business was much smaller than mine."

"Suspicion of murder is a huge credibility buster. Maybe someone wanted to ruin you, Jake."

Frustration knotted his shoulders. "Again, I had no motive. The police know this as well as the public. I passed lie detector tests twice. There was no DNA specifically pointing to me."

Holly thumbed her hair away from her face. "So basically, what you're saying is that you were a logical, traditional suspect because you were the boyfriend or whatever."

"Yep."

She retrieved the pen, then began to doodle. "If you're convinced you know the killer, then the killer must know you."

"Precisely."

"This would mean that the killer knows you're in Guthrie."

"Probably."

"Is that who you think sent the picture?" Holly asked.

"Yes."

"Which brings us back to the list of suspects. You and Dirk."

"Right."

"Jake, what if a woman really did do it?"

"Who, then? Why?"

"Dirk's wife," she said.

"No."

"You said the killer is someone Rayna knew."

"Dirk's wife wouldn't have a motive," Jake said.

"We agree Rayna was killed in a fit of passion, based on the number of stab wounds, most of them wild and random. But what was the reason for the passion? Was it unrequited love? Jealousy? Betrayal? Did someone you know think you and Rayna were the real deal and killed her to eliminate the competition?"

"Tina Nolan was kind of a problem for a while, but I haven't seen her in several months."

Holly wrote the name down.

"Who is she?"

"An ex-employee. A secretary. She did think Rayna and I were an item, even though I told her otherwise."

"Why did it matter to her?"

"I asked Tina to meet some clients for me one night at a restaurant. I was gonna be late. Dinner went well. Another situation came up and she helped me out again."

"Where was Rayna each time?"

"Out of town. Tina thought I was hitting on her, using the excuse that Rayna was unavailable."

"You weren't hitting on her."

"No. Rayna would call, Tina wouldn't pass on the message. I'd work late, Tina would work late. One night she invited me to her apartment. I declined. It was downhill after that."

"You fired her. Tina didn't take legal action against you for letting her go?"

"Surprisingly, no."

Holly put the pen down. "Sounds to me like Tina loved you."

"In some twisted fatal attraction way, you mean? I find it hard to believe since Rayna never mentioned any more problems after Tina was fired."

"What about Rayna?" Holly asked. "Did she hear from Tina?"

"If she was having trouble, she never mentioned it."

"What do you think happened to Tina?"

"I have no idea, but believe me, Holly, I'm gonna find out."

Jake stood, drawing her to him as he did. She pressed her cheek against his chest, aware more now than ever that the man who held her was not a violent man, but there was, she realized, violence in him. Drenched in mystery, hell-bent on revenge, Jake Fishbone had captured her heart.

Eight

The next day was muggy, the air wet, clouds thick and rolling over a sky that wasn't quite blue. The heavy, wet air suited Jake's black mood. He felt rough, edgy.

Someone knocked on the door. Hard.

The guy on the other side had a sturdy face, wide and mean. Not as tall as Jake, but the man's clothes fit him like muscle to bone. His eyes gave away his identity. It was Holly's brother.

Jake made a sound that barely passed for a laugh, even as he readied himself for a battle of words. If the man had really wanted to fight, he'd have stayed outside where there was more room to move around.

"She'll be ticked if we fight," Jake said.

"That won't stop me."

Jake's smile was nasty. "Come in."

Holly's brother entered, but didn't sit down. "Hurt her, Fishbone, and you're a dead man."

"Original."

The man drilled Jake with a stare. "Give me a reason to do what I came here to do."

Jake rolled his shoulders. His furniture wasn't new and there weren't a lot of knickknacks on the shelves, but it all went together pretty well. He hated to bust things up if he didn't have to.

"Listen," he said, "I'm not here to hurt your sister."

It took a full minute, but they did sit down. Their bodies remained tight, their legs spread wide, feet firmly planted on the floor, backs straight, glares going blow for blow.

"Holly doesn't know I'm here."

Jake wasn't surprised. "Figured that."

"God, I'm tempted," the other man said, his fingers flexing.

Jake shrugged. "Do what you gotta do."

Briefly, the man glanced about the room, his astute gaze focusing on a birdhouse under construction. His shoulders relaxed, as did his fingers and wrists. There were five similar houses stacked against a wall, tools on the coffee table, a wrench on the floor. He recognized busywork when he saw it. Jake was going nuts.

"Start at the top, Fishbone. Leave nothing out."

Jake narrowed his eyes.

"So you can compare what you think you know to what I actually say?"

"The top."

Jake told Holly's brother what he knew, what he suspected, why he'd chosen Guthrie for his sabbatical. "I'm sure Kenneth told you this."

"On the phone."

"Which brother are you?" Jake asked.

"I'll ask the questions."

"Nerve must run in your family."

"We're concerned about Holly," her brother said.

"Understandable."

"When Holly asked us to keep our distance, we wondered how much control you have over her."

"Very little."

"That's what Daisy said."

"And Kenneth?"

"He thinks you're the one in danger."

"I keep a low profile around town, especially when I'm with Holly. She likes to stop and visit with people."

"That's the other thing—she isn't doing stuff she normally does."

"Are you referring to her spending time with her usual friends?"

"Yes, they've complained."

Jake's shrug showed he didn't consider this a problem. Holly didn't live for her friends, she lived for herself, which is why she'd told her family to let her do her own thing. "Business is up at Yesterday Is Here Today," he said.

"Because her friends want to keep tabs on her."

"On me," Jake corrected.

"That, too."

There was another twenty seconds of silence, but this time the air inside the house wasn't as thick as the air outside. The men were a long way from being cordial, but at least the appropriate threats and responses had been made. If Holly was hurt in any way, Jake understood he'd suffer bodily harm.

"I won't tell Holly you were here."

"Thanks."

"No problem."

"Understand this, Fishbone, me and Holly are close, real close. If she was truly scared, she'd have called me."

"I take it she didn't call you," Jake said.

The man gritted his teeth before answering. "No."

"What brought you today?"

"The picture of the dead chick."

"She wasn't a chick," Jake said. "Her name was Rayna Holdenbrook."

The man was satisfied Jake had lost some of his cool. They were fighting, just not with their fists. Instead, they measured each other's worth, searching for weak spots, each man finding one. The brother was touchy about Holly; Jake, about Rayna.

"Whoever sent that picture knows more about Holly than I know about you," her brother said.

"And?"

"What happens to you is your business. What happens to Holly is mine."

"So you're here to warn me you'll kill me if she gets hurt, or something along that line. I'm supposed to take you seriously because there won't be any talking if you have to come back. That about cover it?" Jake said.

"Just about."

"Fair enough."

The man rose to leave. "Take care of her, Fishbone," he said.

"I will."

"One thing?" her brother said.

"Yeah?"

"Your sticking close to home is to control your environment, right?"

"The smaller the target and opportunity, the better," Jake said. "I'm not aiming for a bullet, just the truth."

The man presented Jake with a business card— high-quality white stock with raised black script. Nothing fancy, like the man. Sturdy, serviceable, and to the point, again, like the man. "Day or night, Fishbone. Call me."

Jake glanced at the card. "Tell me something, William," he said.

"What?"

"With all Holly's nosey friends and relatives, how'd you plan to sneak into town, lay down the law with me, and leave without being noticed?"

William laughed, a genuine smile on his face. He only looked half as mean, but Jake wasn't fooled. The smile was as temporary as light rain in hundred-degree heat.

"I took the back roads in a rental."

"Parents know you're here?"

"What do you think?"

Jake put the business card in his pants pocket. "If I need help," he said, "I'll call, but even if you came right away, it would take two hours to drive from southern Oklahoma."

William's genuine smile turned genuinely nasty. "I was born here. Raised here. One call from me and you're a dead man. Believe it."

Jake nodded his head once. It was a serious threat coming from a serious man who worked hard for a living, but still made time to check up on his sister. Jake knew William Hunter worked hard, because it was William's tools he used to build the birdhouses that were lined up against his living room wall. Holly's brother owned a small tool and equipment company that catered to crafters and hobbyists.

It was a small world indeed. Glancing at the tools on the coffee table, obviously recognizing his own logo and design, but not commenting on them, William offered his hand to Jake, his grip punishing, one CEO to another.

When Jake opened the door, Holly was standing on the other side, her face cold and hard and beautiful.

Nine

Holly directed her first question to Jake, who watched her as if he didn't trust her not to smack him with her purse, which he estimated was the size of Oklahoma City. "How dare you meet my family behind my back!"

"We all want the same thing, Holly," Jake said when he realized William didn't plan to say a word, "which is to keep you safe."

Holly's stare softened a fraction as she eyed each man. They might not know it, but they were only a year apart in age. Both were driven workaholics, both fierce and loyal and filled with good intentions.

"From now on, you guys," she said, "no secret discussions, especially when I'm the topic."

"Agreed," Jake said.

"Sounds fair," William said at the same time.

Holly put her arms around her brother and hugged him. "I love you," she said. "I can't believe you thought you could sneak into this town without me finding out."

"How did you?" William asked, his features the masculine version of Holly's face, his affection for her touching.

"Mom went to Miss Myrtle's house to get some peaches off her tree." Her tone said, *you idiot.*

William laughed softly, Holly joining him.

"Okay," Jake said, "clue me in on what's so funny."

William supplied the answer.

"As a kid, I once told Mom that the best peaches in the world came from Miss Myrtle's backyard, which I robbed as often as possible."

Jake grinned.

"Don't tell me your mother sent you over here to rip a new hole in my face while she made you a peach pie?"

William smiled. "Fried pies," he said. "She's making me fried pies."

"He's addicted," Holly said.

Jake nodded sagely. He was addicted to his mother's meat loaf and mashed potatoes with shredded cheddar and sour cream. "I understand."

The three stared at each other in quiet communion.

"Well," William said, "I'd better see Mom and Dad."

Holly was dismayed. She hated spending only a few minutes with her brother when she usually only saw him during the holidays. "You're leaving this soon?" she asked.

"In and out was all I could manage today meeting-wise. Sorry, sis."

The siblings hugged, the men shaking hands without crushing any bones.

"Just think," Holly said. "If Miss Myrtle hadn't told Miss Tilly about the peaches, I would have missed this."

"Missed what?" Jake asked.

"Big brother William backing down."

"So, you knew he was planning to kill me?" Jake said.

Holly made a teasing face. Her brother had too much to lose to actually murder Jake. "William only would've done it if you hadn't cut the mustard. Your face isn't smashed, so I guess you passed his test."

Jake opened his mouth and closed it. He knew when to quit.

As Holly walked William to the car, Jake realized how close her brother had come to adding fuel to a situation that was easy to lose control of. It couldn't happen again. He'd been caught off guard and the other man knew it.

He couldn't afford that type of mistake. If there was constant infighting between him and Holly and their immediate circle, they'd never figure out who killed Rayna Holdenbrook. They'd be too busy name-calling and back-stabbing.

As Holly returned to Jake, she squelched her disturbed feelings about her brother's intrusion. She wasn't surprised he'd come to Guthrie. Of all her siblings they were the closest. Ever watchful, ever protective, William had ignored her request to be left alone.

It was natural for her family to choose him to represent them. She had requested her own space and had received it, however grudgingly given. She loved William, loved them all, and was comforted by their unified support.

She needed it for strength, just as Jake needed her for hope. She couldn't, in all good conscience, turn away from him, even though the people closest to her, especially her family, would feel relieved if she walked away.

Jake expected her to leave, she saw it in his eyes. William's presence guaranteed she'd make a safe and final escape. What she wanted to escape was the predictability of her everyday life, her motive for being with him.

Her chance for a special kind of happiness was

here, today, now. She lifted her right hand, stretched the smooth palm toward Jake, who took it, drawing her to his side in quiet triumph.

Holly shared his joy. He could have wrung her neck the other day, but he hadn't. He could have broken her car window or even her face, but he hadn't. He wanted her because he sensed what her heart was figuring out for the first time, that they were falling in love.

Her rational self said that love couldn't come this soon. No, not true love. But the beginnings of love could come this soon, and it had.

Jake wasn't a man a woman could easily forget. Embattled, embittered, in unfamiliar territory, he was the best kind of man, the kind of man who risked his all to be all. He was Rayna Holdenbrook's hero, a man willing to sacrifice his honor, his name, his future in pursuit of the only truth that would lead to justice, and for this, Holly was jealous.

How could she tell William, her family, her friends that she envied an enigma, a woman so strong, so unique, her personality had survived a sudden and violent death? How could she admit she wanted to be treasured the way Jake had treasured Rayna?

Only Holly's desire for Jake ran deeper than simple affection. She wanted more than his respect, more than his friendship, or even his naked body. She wanted the one thing Rayna had never received, which was Jake Fishbone's heart.

Ten

A week later

Jake stood behind Holly in the lace shop, his hands kneading her upper body as she savored a few minutes of quiet time between customers that afternoon.

He smelled wonderful to her, his cologne reminding her of woods and spice, an appropriate scent, she felt, for a man who created custom homes and organic food for backyard birds.

He had arrived unexpectedly, to catch her reaching the end of her afternoon snack, a colorful concoction of cold mandarin oranges, fresh banana slices, golden raisins, and a sprinkle of chopped pecans. She'd tossed the fruit salad with vanilla yogurt. The simple salad was a light, filling meal that helped her keep her figure in shape on days like this, when she felt like pigging out.

She lolled her head back against his chest. Since their long conversations about the murder investigation, an easy vibe of simple companionship permeated their current time together.

"What will your customers say if they walk in here while you're moaning like that?" he asked with a smile.

Holly moaned again. "Whoever comes in will ask

me to move over, then tell you to pick up where you left off."

He continued to massage her neck and shoulders. Often, when he worked, he wished for someone to ease the ache his own torso acquired when he was stationary at his desk for long hours, unaware of how quickly time passed.

Rayna had sometimes done this for him when she surprised him at work on occasion, simply to shoot the breeze. Jake hadn't realized until after her death how much time he and Rayna had spent together that wasn't planned.

He also hadn't fully appreciated Rayna's dry humor, her no-strings friendship until after her death. He wouldn't take Holly for granted, not in that way, not in any way if he could avoid it.

She was leaning pretty hard against him now, trusting him, and yes, falling deeper in love, as he was falling deeper in love with her.

His chuckle was deep, masculine, and territorial. There, in the becoming background of her shop, Holly was exquisite, and he had his hands upon her, her continuing faith in him a gift he treasured.

"Maybe I should lock the front door, then pick up where we left off somewhere more private."

She laughed. "Is that a threat or a promise?"

She was ready for more, a sensual study of the man who held center stage in her waking thoughts, her nighttime dreams. She felt as if she'd known him for months instead of weeks. She tried not to think that his sabbatical would eventually reach an end.

The murder investigation accelerated the intensity level of their relationship; however, Jake's contemplative pace kept them on an even keel. He was taking his time with her, making sure she wanted the same steps forward he did and at the same time. Neither of them could afford second thoughts or regrets.

His body hummed with desire for her, the sensation enhanced by his nearness to her body, her scent, her very personality. Sexual abstinence only heightened the suspense of knowing her completely.

"It's a promise," he vowed.

She pulled her shoulders away from him, stood, and arched her back.

"We'd better stop. As much as I'd like to close early so we can play for real, I'd better do some stocking or dusting or something."

They shared something else, he discovered, a passion for their trade.

"How did you get into the lace business, Holly?"

"My old baby-sitter did it as a hobby. To keep me quiet, she'd have me help her with the easy parts of the process wherever possible. I enjoyed it, and kept at it, learning more and more about technique as I went along. Before I knew it, her hobby had turned into a part-time business and I had become her part-time employee."

"And here you are."

"Yes. My old sitter doesn't make lace or restore it now because of rheumatoid arthritis restrictions, but she advises me on sticky problems that I need to solve. Some customers bring me new lace that they want antiqued to look as if it's old. That part of the business is actually growing."

"Your work is as quirky as mine."

"How so?"

He pulled the stool that matched hers a bit closer, a giant of a man trying to get comfortable in a set of rooms dedicated to the survival of a select and dying art form, an art dominated by women. With the backdrop of fine old lace, shades of mocha, cream, gold, and wine, he looked more rugged than he did on the day they first met.

"I make birdhouses and bird food for hobbyists, something I consider a service-oriented business geared toward conservationists. You repair lace for hobbyists, something you consider a service to those people dedicated to a lost art."

The bell above the door rang, the sound announcing the arrival of the FedEx driver with a shipment of thread. After the driver left, Holly slipped the package under the service counter.

She picked up the conversation where they'd left off, glad for the unusually solemn late afternoon. On days like this, she believed in destiny, that every moment had already been designed through the workings of a master plan. She was glad Jake was part of the plan, part of her happiness.

"I never told you I felt that way about my lace business."

As an entrepreneur who remembered the days when his business was small, Jake understood that because Yesterday Is Here Today was slow now, it didn't mean Holly's business was slow every afternoon. She was too relaxed to truly be worried about the quiet, which they each were inclined to nurse along.

"The level of your commitment shows in the quality of the work you do. Your maximum is also your minimum."

Holly angled her head to the side, her gaze sweeping the hard bone of his jaw, the lips she longed to kiss, and would, if her business didn't have a huge window, one that faced the main street. "That's a funny way of putting it," she said.

He smiled again.

"I wouldn't call you a perfectionist, but rather a realist."

And he was a man who thought ahead. He planned to stop at Homeland, the closest grocery store on his way home, in order to buy strawberries, bananas, golden raisins, chopped pecans, and vanilla yogurt to serve Holly when she came to visit him again, this time for dinner, a meal he'd prepare himself.

"A realist, huh? That's a new one."

"I'll make dinner tonight. Something light."

She wondered from the look on his face if she was dinner, and if she was, she didn't care. It was a wild whim to carve space for herself in his troubled world, and yet there was no other world she'd rather be in.

"Dinner sounds great." No crowds, no fuss, and total privacy, just what she often preferred because she usually dealt with people all day, every day.

By moving to Guthrie, away from Blue Springs, Jake ascribed to the easy living that grounded and nurtured her. Her work was simple, artistic, with only a two-mile commute from home.

Her friendships were durable, old, and comforting, like the lace. She was close to her family, long-standing members of the Guthrie citizenry. Perhaps she was the key to the success he'd find in her world, in Logan County, home of the Hunter family since the Land Run of 1889. Into this life, she had welcomed him.

Jake's legs sprawled out in front of him. They were long, heavy, and muscular, but his thighs were what drew her attention. She imagined them pressed against hers while they made love. The thought of having sex with him soon quickened her breath.

"Are you having much trouble fitting into the town, Jake?"

"Not really. Once people know I'm Daisy's cousin, they crank up the volume on being friendly. I have no true complaints on that score."

"Have you notified the Blue Springs authorities about me getting Rayna's picture in the mail?"

"I did."

She shivered a little, as if menace waited for them both just beyond the glass door. "I want to forget how dangerous this all is, but I shouldn't do that, should I?"

He pulled her into his arms and held her close, two hearts beating in rhythm, two hearts falling further in love.

"Don't forget, Holly, we're talking about murder."

The bell on the door rang.

"Well," Cinnamon Hartfeld said. "What have we here?"

Holly groaned in dismay. Cinnamon's smile was coy, her words bearing a gossipy quality that told her that as soon as Jake left, there was going to be a round of twenty questions to answer.

Eleven

Rayna's business partner, Dirk Adams, stopped at Arby's on Highway 33 in order to regroup. As far as he was concerned, Guthrie, Oklahoma, was a hole-in-the-wall town. The bugs were huge, the air was humid, and the wind blew grit in his eyes.

He couldn't understand why a successful business-man like Jake Fishbone would choose to live in a place that probably didn't have Starbucks. At the moment, he'd kill for a cup of espresso and a long, hot shower.

Dirk's life had been a total disaster since Rayna's murder. The Blue Springs police hadn't ruled him out as a suspect, because he was the last person they believed had seen her alive. He knew this wasn't true, because he hadn't been the one to kill her.

Contrary to what many people suspected, he and Rayna were never lovers. If he hadn't had such a good alibi for the time of her death, he'd be in jail. He'd been able to produce a store receipt for the hour police estimated she'd been murdered.

He could have killed her, but there hadn't been much time between the documented purchase and his return home to present his gift of silk lingerie to his wife of thirteen turbulent years.

The evening marked the anniversary of the day

they'd met, only his wife hadn't remembered and they had fought, the reason she was able to add credibility to his alibi. She remembered the fight because it had interrupted her favorite reality show.

Still, there had been time to kill Rayna.

Maybe Jake was as innocent as he claimed, but then, maybe he wasn't. Maybe he wanted people to think he was in Guthrie to clear his head, but in truth he might be escaping the tight scrutiny of a public who wasn't convinced he hadn't killed one of the darlings of Blue Springs, Arkansas.

Busy brooding, Dirk was surprised to find a young woman taking a seat across from him. The woman's perfume reminded him of a scent familiar to him because Rayna had worn it. Rayna, dear Rayna, how he missed her.

"Hey," he said, "don't I know you or something?"

"Or something?" she asked, haughty.

"Yeah, I mean, haven't we met before?"

The woman was in her late twenties, her body slim, tender, and ripe, only he wasn't seriously interested. Little had interested him since Rayna's death. Rayna's murder, he corrected. God, he still couldn't believe it. Not Rayna.

"No," the intruder said. Her voice sounded defensive, evasive. Angry.

"You sure about that?"

Dealing with hundreds of clients annually, as well as attending related networking events, Dirk had trouble remembering names, sometimes even faces. But when it came to women, he remembered scent, color, shape, and often the way a woman walked, which is why some people frequently suspected him of various affairs. In truth, he loved his wife, which is why he spoiled her, even on the anniversary she had failed to remember.

Again, Dirk looked at the woman in front of him. There was something familiar. Yes, there was that smell, but there was also the arrogant way she carried her shoulders, confident, defiant, her own woman.

This woman didn't wear her hair in the chic way Rayna used to. This woman wore thick black braids that twisted from her widow's peak to the top of her behind.

"I'm positive, Mr. . . ."

"Dirk, just call me Dirk."

"Well, Just Call Me Dirk," she said, "my name's Nola."

A thick-shouldered man with average features, Dirk Adams drew people to him the way bronze statuary garnered attention at parks, in plazas, and in lobbies of corporate America. He exuded intelligence, his overall physical package striking enough to warrant second glances from attractive women, a trait he shared with Jake.

Dirk spoke well, traveled well, entertained when necessary with a skill acquired from extensive practice. He knew how to work the business system, how to assess and manipulate people into giving him what he wanted, just like Jake. Rayna had often teased Jake about being Dirk's twin.

Dirk was tired from traveling when he first arrived into Guthrie, but now that he'd wolfed down a turkey sandwich, he felt better. This woman intrigued him, a déjà vu in progress. He just wished he had a shot of espresso.

Nola recognized an exhausted man when she saw one. Exhausted men didn't pay attention to details. He didn't question the way she'd appeared across from him, alone, a matching turkey sandwich in hand, as if they were a couple.

To the casual observer, they were just that, a couple. This observation was her intention. She also wanted to keep him off guard. A hungry, exhausted man was far easier to manipulate than a rested one. Rested men held tighter to their wits and their wallets. This man required a second wind.

"Where are you staying?" she asked.

His face was skeptical. "Look," he said, "I want to be left alone."

She carried on as if his tone had been kind. It hadn't been. If she wasn't careful, he'd leave before she was ready for him to move on. He suited her secret agenda. All she needed to do was relax.

Nola crumpled both their used papers, putting all the remains on her serving tray. She slid the refuse pile to the right side of the table.

His eyes sharpened their focus. Top executives were rarely foolish men. "What do you want?"

"You."

Dirk stretched a hand for the refuse pile, clearly ready to vacate the table in order to handle his business, but she stayed him with a lavender-painted fingernail, an index finger with hot-pink stripes. Momentarily taken aback, he spoke slowly, as if to be certain there would be no misunderstanding.

"I'm not old-fashioned, Nola, but I'm man enough to do my own picking and asking. I don't like forward women."

She laughed, recognizing the lie for what it was, an attempt to be rid of her. It was a lie because she had no physical power to stop him. She had only the power of suggestion, the subtle context of innuendo.

Experienced women knew how to stroke in all the right places, egos being tops on the list.

"Honey, you really are too sweet," she said, her voice a phony saccharin concoction all its own. "I mean, I knew you were kind of different and that you weren't from around here. You kept looking out the windows like maybe you were expecting company, only nobody came, so I sat down."

His silence gave nothing away, but she knew what he was thinking, that he sat across from her wondering how he'd managed to sit with a woman he didn't know in a town where he'd never been.

She angled her oval-shaped face to one side, her long braids dangling against her left shoulder, bare except for the small tattoo, a red heart wrapped in pastel ribbon, its edges fluttering in the breeze.

"You remind me of a guy I just met," she said. "His name's Jake Fishbone and he sticks out around here the same way you do."

Dirk stood, threw the trash away, and came back to the table. Dark eyes glittering with distrust, nostrils filled with the scent of Rayna, he wondered if the chance meeting with this gabby ingénue was in fact a setup of some sort, but he resisted the urge to glance over his shoulder to see if Jake was there watching him.

The woman remained interesting to him. Her expensive jeans and top did wonders for her figure. She was strong and slightly muscular. She was tall, almost five feet nine inches. Her skin was smooth and dark, the makeup expertly applied. Yes, the come-on could very well be a setup.

Nola met his open skepticism head-on, the way she did most of her problems. She didn't feel there was a mystery to success. Success was all about discipline and desire. Desire meant establishing the want, discipline meant taking the steps to get from simple want to total possession.

"I know a place where you can stay," she offered.

Her tactic surprised him. She could be setting him up for Jake, or she could be after him for herself. The possible motives for their meeting were a puzzle he didn't mind playing with, at least for now.

Mentioning Jake Fishbone kept his mouth on her hook. What he needed was more information, and he wouldn't get that if he took off in a rush. He had a plan, too, a flexible plan, with one goal: the truth about who killed Rayna.

"I didn't say I need a place to stay."

For the first time since their encounter, she relaxed. He wasn't running, he was hunting, only he didn't know what she knew. He didn't know he was being followed. He'd even stopped wondering if they'd met somewhere. It was all right to leave a man wondering, to leave him thinking about what might happen next.

"Educated guess."

"All right," he said, "I'll bite. Where do you recommend?"

He already knew there were three close, convenient choices for hotels, all less than five minutes from where he sat. He could choose the Best Western, the Interstate Motel, or the Sleep Inn. Because he wanted to stay light, he didn't have much luggage, just a large duffel bag with the essentials, a briefcase with files regarding Rayna.

"My place."

Dirk got up from the table, stood above her, and stared, oblivious of the pointed looks he received from several patrons, curious people thinking that perhaps he and Nola were sharing a lovers' spat.

He hadn't realized they'd been leaning toward each other, voices low, attention riveted one upon the other. He took a serious assessment of his options. Here sat a bold-minded woman who wanted to take him home.

If he went home with her, he wouldn't have to worry about lodging. Not having a registered place to stay, such as a hotel, would reduce his paper trail, one reason he was paying his expenditures in cash.

She was also a solid information source in the form of a tour guide, a navigator in unknown territory. The main problem with Nola was the trust factor. How could he trust a woman he only just met? Once his business was finished in Guthrie, how could he leave her behind to act as a witness to his dealings in town? She posed a problem.

He took her arm, led her outside. He'd done a brief study of Guthrie before taking this trip. A national historic landmark, the town was known for its refurbished Victorian buildings.

If he wasn't here, on the verge of committing murder to avenge the killing of Rayna, he'd be interested in touring the downtown district, a place he'd checked out on the Internet before hitting the road. He'd stay at a bed-and-breakfast instead of a highway motel. He'd bring his wife, rekindle the flame of her desire, but it was Rayna who needed him now. She needed him to avenge her.

"Do you live alone?" he asked.

Her laugh was sly and oily, too short to be taken seriously. "I like men who speak their minds. Yes, I do."

His eyes scanned the busy parking lot, the Brahm's eatery, the Love's gas station, the vacant field waiting to be stocked with other commercial businesses, and stayed on course with his commitment. He wanted Jake Fishbone.

"I'll follow you in my car."

Nola managed to curtail her excitement. She had made use of her opportunity to sit with him, had accomplished her goal to trap and use him. She wouldn't allow herself to feel swayed by his daring, his ability to flex with the moment.

She liked men who knew when to play it safe, when to cut loose and take chances. She noticed he hadn't asked about Jake Fishbone, and he should have, because the name Fishbone was unusual. This meant he suspected her motive for squeezing her tight jeans into the booth with him at Arby's.

"Great," she said. "How long you planning on staying?"

"Long enough."

She looked him up and down, but her eyes gave nothing away. To give nothing away was all about keeping conversation to the minimum. She didn't gossip. She didn't ask questions that didn't relate to her agenda. Jake Fishbone was her agenda. Dirk Adams was her alibi. She simply had to take her time to get what she wanted.

"I'm ready." Her little laugh was silk and satin over steel.

He laughed, too, but the sound of it was low and full of secrets. It was she who had opened herself up to him, she who had opened the door to corruption, to opportunity, to his mission to seek, then destroy Jake Fishbone.

Dirk was too much of a businessman not to recognize a strategic plan in the works. The braids didn't match the corporate light in her eyes. He'd worked with enough corporate women to know one when he saw one. In his experience, they were harder, more aggressive, more focused than men, and they had tougher egos. Rayna and his own selfish wife had taught him that much.

"Don't get me wrong, Just Call Me Dirk, I'm not looking to get hurt," she said, "but I'm not looking for promises either. When it's time for you to go, I'll let you know."

"Then," he said, "so be it."

His late-model sedan left the Arby's parking lot in a slow glide, as he followed her outdated economy car, a tan one with a dent on the right side. They drove west on Highway 33, which became Noble Avenue.

They made a right on Pine, then turned right into a small apartment complex located directly across from a baseball field. As soon as Dirk pulled into the parking lot, he lost his anonymity.

Right away, a woman with two children struck up a conversation about the weather, then politely asked him for his name.

Twelve

Holly folded her arms across her chest. She was a formidable woman despite her deceptively feminine look in floral capri pants and a bright yellow shirt with ruffles along the neck and wrists. She wore rose-colored jewels around her neck, dangling from her ears, on her fingers and right ankle. Her skimpy rope sandals were hot pink, another favorite color of Rayna's, only Holly didn't know it.

"That's bull, Jake. We all worry about what other people think."

As the tension in his body increased, Jake wanted action, not conversation. He left the kitchen and walked toward the living room to avoid Holly's probing. He stopped at the living room window and was stunned to see a man on the golf course spying on him with binoculars.

"What the—"

Jake shot out of the house without a word to Holly or concern for his own safety. "Hey! Hey, you!" he yelled.

Holly ran after him. This was Guthrie. Nothing ever happened in Guthrie!

She was three steps behind Jake as he dashed across his front lawn to the golf course across the street. Hot diggity damn! She couldn't wait to tell Zenith and Cinnamon about her escapade. That is, if she lived to tell the tale.

They ran across Midwest Boulevard, scrambled through native trees, and hurtled over the fairway where everyone looked on in shock. Holly knew half a dozen people on the golf course, and half of those people would be in the shop the next day asking her what the hell she was doing racing across the greens on the heels of a screaming maniac.

She caught up with Jake just as Spud Gurber did. Spud's civilian clothes didn't diminish his air of authority as he planted his body like a wall in front of Jake.

Jake knew when to cut his losses. He stopped to catch his breath and watched his quarry get clean away. If he weren't so honorable, he'd have decked the golfer blocking his way in order to continue the footrace.

But this was Guthrie, a small town full of observant people. Jake was sure someone on the golf course could provide a good description of the guy with the binoculars. All Jake had to do was control his temper and avoid a fight with the man standing in front of him. This was a private golf course and he was trespassing.

Jake wasn't surprised the golfer was someone Holly knew well. She placed her hand on the stranger's biceps before the two men came to blows. A fight between them would be nasty, regardless of who won.

"Spud," she said. "We can explain."

An off-duty cop, Spud Gurber kept his eyes on the man in front of him trying to catch his breath.

"Sure, you can explain, my little chili pepper."

Jake was confounded by the slow drawl and the friendly exchange between Holly and the golfer. But he didn't shift his glance. He was busy sizing up the man who was doing the same to him. Spud Gurber was a threat. But then, so was he.

Jake's voice was hard. "Little what?"

"Chili pepper," Spud said, knowing his familiarity pushed Jake's buttons. "Girl's always in the hot sauce makin' it hotter."

Jake looked at Holly. Her hair was wild from their run across the golf course, her feet bare. She was beautiful and he wanted to protect her. He returned his gaze to the stranger. "Who are you?"

Spud's eyes turned to ice. "Man, I'm the one needs to be asking the questions."

Jake was oblivious of Holly's tugging on his arm. He really wanted to punch the toothpick-chomping, slow-talking chump standing before him. "Why should you be the one to ask the questions?"

"I'm a cop," Spud said, a smug look on his face. "You're lucky you ain't in more trouble than you're in right now."

"Oh, yeah?"

Spud's lip curled. "Strange black man chasing another strange black man on country club property ain't likely to drum up positive public support," he said. "Folks recognize me and Chili Pepper here, so you're gittin' some slack."

Spud switched his toothpick from one side of his mouth to the other.

Jake wasn't fooled. This cop was doing more than his duty. The man was hot for Holly, only she wasn't paying him much attention, a satisfying thought. He offered his hand. "I'm Jake Fishbone."

Spud ignored Jake's hand. "Fortunately for y'all, I

was here practicing my swing, which means I got time to talk things over. What I can help with, I'll do."

Holly smiled at him, grateful he wasn't going to embarrass her with a fistfight or some other macho baloney. She didn't know if a fistfight would get Spud in trouble with his superiors or not, but whatever stayed his hand, she was happy for it.

"Thanks, Spud."

Spud looked at Holly as if he wanted to snatch her from Jake's side. "At your service, CP."

Jake looked the cop over. Officer Gurber was more than the country hick he pretended to be. His profession might explain why he hadn't asked Jake what his business was in town. He probably already knew.

After spending several minutes explaining to country club staff what the ruckus was about, the trio headed over to Jake's place. Along the way, Holly's missing sandals turned up. She'd kicked them off as she was running.

Spud managed to maneuver Holly away from Jake so that she was on his left side, and Jake on his right. Spud didn't trust Jake, and Jake didn't trust him, either.

Once they reached Jake's place, the three entered through the back door into the kitchen. Jake pulled out a chair for Spud at the small table, then sat across from him with Holly by his side.

With a nod to Jake that he recognized what all the territorial positioning was about, Spud faced his surly host, matching him glare for glare. He was nobody's fool. Holly could be moved out of the way and the table overturned in two shakes. Spud wanted a reason to hit Jake.

His edge with Holly was their history together. They had a track record that could be superseded, but never erased, which is why he had yet to call Holly by her real name. He wanted Jake to know he was part of her life. In the bigger picture, there was a future for him as well.

He'd been keeping tabs on her ever since he'd heard about the picture she'd received in the mail. Watching her spend time with the very man Kenneth Gunn had been telling him about really rattled Spud. If he hadn't been concentrating on his golf swing, he'd have spotted the man with the binoculars before Jake did.

Maintaining his steely glare, Spud asked, "So, Chili Pepper, tell me what's goin' on." He already knew quite a lot about why Jake was in town. Kenneth had asked him to keep an eye on Holly.

Unaware of the sparring going on between Jake and Spud, Holly explained how she met Jake, which was fine with Spud. He wanted her perspective.

When she finished, Spud said, "Has it occurred to you, CP, that this guy might have an ulterior motive for bein' with you?"

Holly thumbed her hair back and scrunched her face up. "Oh, please."

"Maybe Fishbone agreed to meet you because he wants to use you."

"Don't be silly, Spud."

"He could've sent the picture of that girl to you himself."

Holly couldn't believe what was happening. Things were getting too wild for her, too out of control. She liked to keep her life simple. "Stop it, Spud. Just stop it."

Spud ignored her. He turned to speak to Jake, who was fuming at Spud's accusations.

"I'd be interested in knowing how you plan to keep Holly safe. You've been accused of murder. Someone sent her a picture to warn her about you. A man spied on you with binoculars. What's next?"

Jake forced himself to stay calm. His body screamed with tension. "Careful, Gurber. You lost your hick drawl."

Holly hit the table with her fist. "Cut it out! Both of you!"

Spud kept his eyes on Jake. "Jake Fishbone is a suspect in a murder investigation, Holly. He hasn't been ruled out for a reason. He might be guilty."

"It was probably the real killer who was spying on him," she said.

Spud spoke with care. "Maybe Fishbone is being followed. Maybe somebody is sure this arrogant bastard is really guilty but ain't got the facts to prove it."

Holly punched him in the arm. "Spud!"

But the cop kept talking. "What better way to stay up on a murder investigation than to give a private detective a sob story that keeps him in the loop? Many a killer has worked with the police as a way to git close to his own crime without gittin' caught."

"I believe Jake is innocent," Holly said.

Spud chewed his toothpick, his eyes glistening with rage. "Nobody's innocent, Holly. Nobody at all."

Jake stood and so did Holly. She planned to stick with him, at least for now. Smart women considered all of their options. Holly might be mad at Spud, but she trusted him. She would listen to his words of caution and reason. She'd reach her own conclusions.

Jake understood this about Holly and was relieved. They still had a chance for happiness. "Call me,

Gurber, if you find something out about the guy we chased."

Spud watched Holly move to stand beside Jake, and for a minute he couldn't see straight. "Oh, I'm gonna find somethin' out, Fishbone. Believe it."

Thirteen

Holly returned home to think. She hadn't been as oblivious of the subtle fighting between Jake and Spud as they had suspected. She couldn't believe she'd never realized Spud Gurber wanted her to himself. He'd always been kind to her, protective of her. But never had he been so aggressive about his desire to keep her close.

Consequently, she'd taken him for granted, the way she tended to treat many of the people she saw on a regular basis, especially those she'd known most of her life. Spud was easy to trust. But today, his real motive had been revealed. He wanted her for more than friendship.

As much as she cared for Spud, it was Jake she wanted. Jake had shown no fear when he realized someone had been spying on them. He had been equally fearless when confronted by Spud. She found his tough attitude exciting. His possessive manner commanded her attention, as if he were staking a claim to her, as if he had the right to claim her.

Like Jake, she hadn't been fooled by Spud's country hick act. Spud had a law degree. With his normally good judgment clouded by jealousy, he posed a serious threat to her budding romance. Her relationship with

Jake didn't need more pressure. This is why she'd wanted her family and friends to give her the space she needed to make up her mind about Jake on her own.

She had always trusted Spud, but his territorial behavior made him a problem. She had little reason to trust Jake, but his determination to solve his friend's murder inspired her. Faced with the unsolved murder of one of her own friends, she wasn't sure she'd be as committed.

Had Jake not been there, she might easily have given Spud another look, especially if he'd been this aggressive. He was a man in power and powerful men turned her on. And yet, it had been Jake's struggle to hang on to his self-control that she found the most attractive. He could have argued with Spud, but he'd resisted the impulse.

He'd found a better way to use his heightened energy, and that had been to make love. She'd made love before, but not with such passion. Sex with Jake Fishbone would be addictive. Already, she wanted more.

Before she met Jake, Holly had been going to the movies with her girlfriends. Now she barely had time to return their phone calls. Cinnamon Hartfeld had finally stopped calling her and started banging on her door in order to find out what Holly had been up to with the mysterious Jacob Fishbone.

Even though Cinnamon had a big mouth, Holly had given her friend the general rundown of what was going on in her life—that she didn't have time for the mall or the movies because she was tied up in a slow-burning romance.

Of course, Cinnamon, with her big mouth, couldn't wait to spread the news, which cut down on the phone calls and increased the traffic in Holly's shop. While angling for gossip, some of the nosey snoops wound up buying lace, partly to clear their conscience and partly because they genuinely liked the merchandise.

Holly was seriously considering whether to put the word out about the murder investigation. There was no telling what her gossipy friends might turn up. She made a mental note to run her idea by Jake the next time she saw him.

An hour later, she had her chance when he knocked on her door. She opened it right away.

"Got any more men in your life you want to tell me about?"

She grinned, mostly because of the way he looked at her, like a juicy red strawberry dunked in whipped cream. "Not that I know of. Besides, Spud and I are just friends."

"Tell him that."

She sensed Jake wanted to grab her up and carry her off to a secret hideaway. She'd let him, too, if the place had a brass bed, plump pillows, and a fan to cool the perspiration from her skin after they made love.

As if he read her mind, Jake pulled her close and kissed her. Instead of thinking about who might have killed Rayna, he'd been thinking about driving over to see Holly. Staring out of his living room window, he noticed Spud Gurber parked in a patrol car on the street in front of his house. Without thinking his actions through, he walked outside, nodded his head to acknowledge Spud, then climbed into his Jeep.

Holly had opened her door as if she'd been expecting him. She held on to him now as if she might never let him go. She eased the pain of his grief every time she welcomed him into her life with a smile on her lovely face.

Lifting her into his arms, Jake kicked the door shut. As soon as it closed, Spud Gurber leaned on his car horn. The sound was childish, obnoxious, and effective. Holly couldn't ignore it. Spud had a point. Jake was still a murder suspect.

Holly cleared her throat. Visions of Jake's sculpted brown chest and chocolate nipples filled her mind. But in order to have a successful relationship, she had to help him clear his name.

"I thought about asking a couple of my friends to help with the investigation, Jake. Maybe keep an eye out for anything unusual. We don't have any leads. We haven't tracked down any suspects. All we've done is talk about it. I mean, it's only been a short while, but we don't have much more to go on than when we started."

"That's debatable," Jake said. "Someone did spy on me with binoculars." His suspicions about being followed had been confirmed.

"Aren't murders solved through careful analysis of clues?" Holly went on. "Don't forget, we don't have any new information."

"Did it ever occur to you, Holly, that I might have set myself up as bait?"

"No, but it obviously worked since we caught that man watching you. Do you think he might be Rayna's killer?"

"I don't know. We can't be too careful, Holly. My mind is split between Rayna, her killer, my business, and you. It's dangerous for you to be involved at all. Don't you understand that someone out there is stalking me? They're watching you. Somebody out there wants to see me dead or in jail. Don't you understand how serious this is?"

Holly glared at him. "Don't insult me, okay? I know this is for real and all, but enough people at the golf course saw that guy to remember him later. Maybe someone saw him earlier in the day. For all you know, he could have found out where you lived by talking to somebody in town. I mean, you're not exactly a secret around here anymore."

"True."

"On the subject of secrets," Holly said. "I think I *will* tell everything I know to the girls. They ought to be able to help."

"No!"

"Don't yell at me because your life's in such a mess. I'd be nuts to tell Spud Gurber to mind his own business. As nosey and blabbermouthed as Cinnamon Hartfeld is, she's as good as gold. She'll have her friends doing more drive-bys of this place than the Guthrie police."

"I'm going home and you're coming with me," Jake said.

"Nope."

"I'm thinking of your safety."

"There's always Spud."

"Look, Holly, this situation is becoming a circus."

"As long as you're at my place, the cops and my friends will know it, which means we'll both be better off. You can't be on guard all the time, Jake. My friends and neighbors will look out for me. They'll look out for you too because they trust my judgment."

"I don't like it."

Holly tried to ease his concerns. "I know you feel responsible for me. I appreciate that. Truth is, I'm really scared. But I'm here with you because I want to be. I hate seeing a good man being railroaded."

Jake inhaled deeply. "Before Rayna was killed, I lived a peaceful life. I had my work and there was order. When I had time for a solid relationship with a beautiful woman, I couldn't be bothered. I should let you go. But God forgive me, I can't do it."

"I want you, Jake. This is where I want to be."

"Spud Gurber wishes he'd made his move on you a long time ago," Jake said, as his eyes fell from her face to her breasts. He noticed her nipples were pressing against the flimsy fabric of her dress.

"He and I are just friends, Jake."

"The men in your life are playing for keeps, Holly, and that includes me."

"You're the only man in my life."

"You've got me, Spud, and the guy with the binoculars."

"How do you know that guy wasn't bird-watching or something?"

"He ran."

"Because you chased him."

Hearing a sound outside, Jake opened Holly's door. Spud was sitting in a chair on her front porch. If Holly screamed, even in passion, Spud would use it as an excuse to bust the door down. Jake closed the door. "I want you to come with me," he said.

"Let's not argue about it, okay? I'll go home with you, so you can pack a few things. Let me grab my purse real quick."

"All right, but Spud's gotta go."

As they walked out the front door to his car, Spud was gone. Cinnamon honked her horn and waved as she drove down the street. Daisy was right behind her. Zenith Braxton pulled up to the curb, patiently waiting for Holly to fasten her seat belt in Jake's Jeep.

He laughed as he drove toward home, Zenith on his bumper. "You were right about one thing, Holly."

"What's that?"

"You've got great friends."

Holly linked her fingers with his **and settled in for** the short ride. "Absolutely."

When they reached his home, **Jake realized he** didn't want to fight with Holly anymore. She didn't understand that her being a woman only added fuel to the fire—that he didn't think she could handle herself physically if Rayna's killer caught her alone.

"I can't stand the thought of you getting hurt," he said.

If Holly had known she looked fragile in her dress, she'd have worn jeans and boots. "What's life without risks?" she said.

Jake thought of the people who cared about Holly. "By the time the sun comes up tomorrow, half the town will know what's going on. I may as well have stayed in Arkansas."

"If you had, I might've died of boredom."

Jake took her by the shoulders. He looked as if he couldn't make up his mind if he wanted to shake her or kiss her.

Holly seized the moment. Stepping back, she eased the straps of her dress down her arms. She wore sheer lace panties and a matching bra.

Jake responded with a groan. Crushing her to him, he caressed her soft skin. "You don't play fair."

She reached for the buckle of his jeans.

Lifting her in his arms, Jake carried her to the sofa. "One of these days we're gonna make it to the bedroom."

Holly opened her heart to him, and Jake used his body to thank her.

Outside, Rayna's killer watched as the lights went out.

Fourteen

Dirk Adams was the man Jake had spotted using binoculars to spy on him. He considered himself lucky to have escaped the golf course without getting tackled by Jake or some Good Samaritan. He didn't doubt that Nola, the woman he'd met at Arby's, wanted Jake to suffer, too.

Dirk and Nola had bought wine from Moonfeathers Winery on Midwest Boulevard and were now sipping it from paper cups at her apartment. There were no real cups in the kitchen cupboards, no real dishes either. Everything everywhere was disposable. Her car was a rental. Her life was a rental.

Suddenly, Dirk laughed, the sound a sinister thing in the closed confines of the apartment that Nola continually dusted. He knew she was dusting away fingerprints, constantly, obsessively. Her every gesture was calculated. But the wine made her vulnerable, which was his intention.

"The police were in the complex today," she said. "They were asking if anyone recognized a composite picture of a guy who looked a lot like you."

For the thousandth time, Dirk tried to remember where he'd met Nola. "Tell me the truth," he said. "Who are you?"

She shrugged. "I'm Tina Nolan."

Dirk was surprised she answered him so easily. He was suspicious. "Our meeting at Arby's wasn't an accident, was it?"

"No."

Dirk had been watching Jake's house in Guthrie, wondering if he and Nola were in cahoots together. But she wasn't Nola. She was Tina Nolan, and maybe she'd followed Jake to Guthrie to keep an eye on him herself. "Why are you here?" he asked.

"I know who killed Rayna."

"Was it Jake?"

"No."

Dirk studied Tina Nolan. She wore Rayna's perfume, Obsession. She wore Rayna's favorite color, lavender. "You gave me the wrong name at first because you wanted to protect your identify, right?"

"Right.

"Were you following me to Guthrie or were you already here because you'd followed Jake?"

"I followed Jake. I waited for you."

Dirk enjoyed the challenge Tina presented. The smell of her, the arrogance, were familiar because they reminded him of Rayna. "Did you kill her?" he asked.

"Yes."

Her answer didn't surprise Dirk. The wine had relaxed his body, but his mind was sharp. He hadn't made a success of his advertising business by ignoring the obvious. Tina Nolan was familiar for other reasons, not because of Rayna. "I know who you are," he said.

She laughed a little. "I wondered if she mentioned me."

Dirk poured more wine into their Dixie cups. Tina Nolan was articulate, educated. She moved as if she were used to cocktail parties, fine restaurants, and black-tie affairs. She had once worked for Jake. "Were you jealous of Rayna? Is that why you killed her?"

Tina realized that Dirk was observing the details of her face, her skin, her hair. His eyes were constantly returning to her hair, her widow's peak. This was much like a birthmark, distinctive and unusual. Of course it was her hair he finally remembered.

"She loved Jake," Tina said, realizing too late that she'd drunk more wine that Dirk. He was more clever than she'd given him credit for being.

"You're wrong," he said. "Jake and Rayna were friends."

"No," Tina argued. "Jake wanted her to choose him instead of her job. She never did. I wanted him."

"He didn't want you."

"Only because Rayna kept throwing herself at him."

"Jake and Rayna were friends. Period."

"Jake was mine."

"Jake Fishbone is and always has been a workaholic. I know you were once his secretary and that he asked you to help him with social functions, but that's all Jake's been about since I've known him—a workaholic. Rayna was the same way. They didn't have time for steady partners, which was the key to their success."

"Jake didn't want her."

"He didn't want you, either."

"Rayna—"

"Understood Jake. You killed her for nothing."

"She was in the way," Tina said.

"If anything, it was his job that was in the way."

Tina smiled. "Two birds. One stone."

"You knew about his sabbatical, then?"

"Yes. Eventually I planned to bump into him. Make him see how good I am for him."

"You're crazy."

"And you're stupid."

As it had during the attack on Rayna, Tina's knife appeared as if by magic. Using the element of surprise, she whipped the knife from the small of her back and threw it into the soft hollow of his throat.

An hour later, Tina left the apartment. She said hello to the boy washing his truck outside. She smiled at the children drawing pictures on the sidewalk with colored chalk. She wondered how long it would take for someone to find the dead body of the man who'd tried to dull her mind with wine.

Fifteen

Spud stood on Holly's doorstep, legs wide, arms akimbo. He was off duty. Dressed in jeans, a long-sleeved cotton shirt, scuffed boots, and a straw cowboy hat, he looked like a cross between Joe Cool and a hit man. "I'm not leaving, Fishbone, until I talk to her alone," he said.

Jake stood on Holly's doorstep facing Spud, his legs and arms straddling the doorway. He was dressed in jeans, a short-sleeved cotton top, and scuffed boots. Their similarities were just one more reminder that he was the rugged type that Holly liked to have around. "I'm not leaving her alone with anybody."

Holly sat on the front porch in the glider swing where she usually drank hot tea after work. Today, Jake and Spud were driving her nuts. Spud was taking advantage of the situation by pushing the limits of their friendship. Jake didn't have the right to deny anyone access to her. She was a simple woman with simple needs. She wasn't used to all this drama. "You guys need to get a grip," she said.

The two growled at the same time, "Quiet."

Holly stopped pushing the swing with her feet. "You've got some kind of nerve. Both of you!"

Jake and Spud turned to look at her.

"You guys seem to have forgotten that this is my house. If I had wanted the police, Spud, I'd have called the police. And, Jake, if you're gonna be my bodyguard, you've got to take my needs into consideration."

"Holly," they said in unison. Slightly embarrassed, the two stared at each other, legs wide, arms at their sides, hands balled into fists.

Holly stood up. "This is stupid," she said. "Either come inside the house with me, or you can both go home."

They went inside the house, Holly between them. Once inside, neither man sat down. The tension in the air was a lethal mix of testosterone and old-fashioned hardheadedness. They weren't in the mood to listen. They were fuming, and not about Holly. It was a territorial skirmish that neither was about to back down from.

Disgusted with their flexing, Holly pushed them both into a chair. "Spud," she said. "What's on your mind?"

"I don't want you to be alone with a possible murderer. When he's in here I can't help wondering how you're doin'."

"I appreciate that, Spud, and I understand," she said. "It's important that you respect my decision to help Jake."

Spud didn't press his point. Arguing wasn't going to help him win Holly from Jake. In the short run, it might get her killed. "Okay, Fishbone," he said. "Let's say you're innocent. What then?"

"I'm two months into a three-month sabbatical. In another month I'm due back in Blue Springs. I hope Rayna's murder is solved before I leave here."

"And if it ain't?" Spud said.

Jake looked at Holly. "I've got a business to run."

Holly knew many murder cases remained unsolved, and she doubted the hole Rayna left in Jake's life would ever be filled. But it hurt that he didn't say he wanted to keep seeing her. She was more than half in love with him. "What about us, Jake?"

"I don't know."

Immediately, the tension between Jake and Spud shot up.

"That ain't good enough, Fishbone," Spud said. "You can't just come here and screw up her life, then leave."

"I never promised her anything."

Holly was crushed. "He's right," she told Spud, her voice husky with emotion. "I've always known that Rayna came first."

Spud couldn't stand the pain in Holly's eyes. "I don't think he deserves you. But I'm gonna do everything I can to help Fishbone prove he's innocent."

Jake knew Spud was telling him something. If he didn't commit to Holly before his sabbatical was over, Spud planned to claim her for himself. "I'll give you my case file," he said to the cop.

After Spud left with the file, Jake sat with Holly in the living room. He'd been self-absorbed with his problems, not really taking time to think of what she'd given up to be with him.

He'd put Rayna on a pedestal she hadn't deserved, all because he felt guilty he hadn't been there to save her life. No one could be everywhere. Even if he had been at her house when the killer showed up, their was no guarantee he wouldn't have been killed trying to save her. Holly deserved better, and so did he. There were lives at stake, careers at risk.

Jake drew her into the circle of his arms. "I can't believe how lucky I am."

"What do you mean?" she asked.

"You're so giving that I took you for granted."

"I've given up a lot because I expect a lot in return."

"Like what?"

"The truth," she said. "Are you afraid of commitment?"

"Until Rayna's murder, my passion was my work. Her death was a reality check. I had an excellent career and a lousy love life. Rayna didn't ask for anything more and I didn't offer."

Holly thought of Spud's secret passion for her. "Is your guilt really about missed opportunity?"

"No. What I feel for you is completely different."

"In what way?"

Jake covered her lips with his own.

"Sex is not enough for me," she said. "It's not enough for me that you can't commit until Rayna's murder is solved. That might never happen."

"I want you, Holly. I like being with you. Regardless of what happens in another month, I'd still like to see you. But I'm not making promises I'm not ready to keep."

"At first, all I wanted from you was a good time. When I found out you were in trouble, I wanted to help you. But I've always expected that in return you'd give me your all, starting with honesty. I deserve the best, Jake. I want the best to be you."

"Since meeting you, Holly, I don't feel as overwhelmed by Rayna's death. Faced with losing you to Gurber, I recognized that you mean more to me than a simple diversion. I'm not afraid of commitment, I'm afraid of endangering your life."

She snuggled against him and felt safe. "Spud and Kenneth will help us."

Jake held her close. She felt soft and warm. She smelled wonderful like she always did. "You make me feel alive. Because of your friends, Rayna has a real chance for justice."

For a long while, they said nothing. Rayna's death was the catalyst that brought Jake to Guthrie. Her death had paved the way for this new beginning. But Holly felt she had a choice too, to live life to the fullest.

She hadn't been looking for a husband or a hero, but she knew a good man when she found one. There wasn't a thing wrong with Spud Gurber other than the fact that he didn't ring her bells the way Jake Fishbone did.

"How did you buy Kenneth's place so fast?" she asked.

"Cash. I bought the property at a steal."

"I bet."

"That's irrelevant to the case, Holly."

"Everything matters. You moved here fast. A suspicious person might think you plotted to kill Rayna in advance, then planned your getaway under the pretense of going someplace to lick your wounds."

"Is that what you think?"

"I think Spud is right to question your motives for being here. Maybe if one of my friends was in this situation I'd question your motives, too."

"Why didn't you, Holly?"

Holly remembered seeing Jake the first time. Strong, sexy, and sinewy, he had captured her woman's inner eye. Her eye noticed that his smile came easy, an expression of confidence. He had fine manners and took pride in his appearance. She'd liked him before she knew Daisy was his cousin.

"My first impression of you, Jake, was a good one. Things were going pretty well until somebody sent that picture. You have Daisy and Kenneth's support, and that means a lot to me. Being with you is kind of like going on an adventure. I don't know what's gonna happen, but I can't wait to find out."

"At first, all I could think about was Rayna. Now, all I dream about is you. I'm obsessed with you both and it's driving me crazy."

Holly didn't know what to say. Her eyes were dark with desire, her body readying itself to make love. She licked her lips.

His expression was primitive. He lowered his head, his mouth slanting hard over hers in a kiss that blew Holly's mind. Her skin burned beneath her clothes, her breasts aching and full. Feeling his arousal, she pressed her hips against him. She couldn't walk away from him, not now, maybe never.

Some part of her mind told her to be careful, but she didn't want to listen. She wanted this too bad to stop. Right or wrong, she wanted him.

Jake carried her into the bedroom, his breath harsh with the need to bury himself inside the body he couldn't get out of his mind. As she watched, he stripped himself of his clothes, the cool air a sensual contrast to the heat of his skin.

Holly reached for a condom before she opened her arms to receive him. He nibbled the sides of her neck, the center of her throat as his fingers tested the heat between her thighs. Together, they removed her clothes. But this time it was Holly who controlled their encounter.

She touched every part of his body, front and back, top to bottom, with her lips, her tongue, her teeth and hands. His muscles rippled as she brought him to the edge of fever, then pulled back before the fever broke.

When Holly straddled his body for one final ride, Jake turned the tables by rolling her onto her back. She'd thought the show was almost over, when the games had only just begun.

Jake was tireless. He worked his hips like a machine—hard, fast, and steady. His muscles rippled beneath her hands. His hips bucked against her legs as she used them to pull him tighter against her. Holly came once, twice, then again.

Jake's release came with a roar. Hoarse and thick, his voice sent a pulse of heat through Holly. When she finally opened her eyes, he kissed her deeply, solemnly. And then, the phone rang, and the spell they were under was broken.

Sixteen

Holly allowed the answering machine to pick up. "What a reality check," she said, as she heard Spud's voice asking her to call back. "We'd better get dressed."

In the living room, Holly turned on every light. She wanted everything to be as bright as she could make it. Hope flourished in the light.

She sat beside Jake on the sofa, in easy comfort. For a long while, they said nothing. In silence, they agreed to let the bad blood between Jake and Spud make its way out of the house. What was hope anyway, but forgiveness, and new beginnings?

Rayna's death was the catalyst that brought Jake to Guthrie. Her death had paved the way for this new beginning. But Holly felt she had a choice too, to live life to the fullest. At least she and Jake were on the same page. They were choosing to be happy. They were choosing to be together.

She pulled a pen and a piece of scrap paper from a drawer in the coffee table. She wrote *death of a businesswoman*.

"Dramatic," he said.

She drew a circle, then wrote Rayna's name inside. "Our investigation consists of talk. Period. We can't visit the crime scene. We can't interrogate anyone. We're the *a* in *amateurs*."

"This is where Spud and Kenneth can help," Jake said.

Holly nibbled her pen. "Maybe some of my other friends can help."

Jake was shaking his head before she finished. "It won't work."

"Why?"

"There's something to be said for proceeding with caution, Holly."

"There's something to be said for taking risks, too. I'm taking risks to be with you. But I'd rather do that than do nothing and regret it later."

"Point taken."

"Besides, if my friends and customers feel like they have a stake in the outcome of the investigation, they'll be more vigilant. I bet if more people knew you were in trouble, that guy with the binoculars wouldn't have gotten away. Somebody would've tackled him."

Jake thought about the instant way Spud had come to Holly's aid. "You're probably right."

Holly drew another circle, then wrote the word *binoculars* inside. She connected the circles with a thick blue line. "Mr. Binoculars wasn't too smart, was he?"

"No, he wasn't. I understand that the police were able to get a sketch of him based on the descriptions from witnesses. Chances are good somebody will recognize him if he's still around."

"I bet he's still here. It takes a desperate guy to do what he did. Anybody standing on the golf course with binoculars would be noticed. What he did was risky. But it happened quickly, which was in his favor."

Jake nodded his head. "Between Spud and Kenneth, the local police are taking Rayna's case seriously. I appreciate that. I'm still amazed, Holly, you didn't know how Spud felt about you."

"Well."

Jake laughed. She was nibbling on her bottom lip, something Jake hadn't noticed her do before. "Is that all you can say?"

Holly didn't speak. She didn't know where to begin. Yes, she and Spud had gone out on a date, but she looked at that date the same way she looked at a date with one of her girlfriends. They knew enough of the same people to share gossip and a good conversation.

"Holly?"

"I just can't take him seriously," she went on, as if she hadn't been lost in thought. "He's like my buddy, you know?"

"It's how I felt about Rayna."

The phone rang again. Forgetting she had the answering machine on, Holly picked up the receiver on the second ring. "Hello?"

"Holly, honey, it's Miss Myrtle. I heard you've got some show-and-tell planned for our next lace workshop."

"Show and tell?"

"Yes, honey. You show us this Jake Fishbone and we'll tell you what all we can do to help you solve that case of his."

Holly stifled a groan. "That may not be necessary, Miss Myrtle, but thanks, anyway."

"Honey, we didn't get to help Daisy when she was having trouble with Kenneth, but we're sure gonna help you."

Holly hung up the phone, then turned to look at Jake. "The cat is out of the bag."

"You mean the whole town knows?"

"Maybe not the whole town, but enough for you to forget about your privacy."

"We'll deal with it."

"That's not all though. The lace shop ladies have decided to pitch in and help us out. They're a runaway freight train we can't stop."

His eyes crinkled at the corners as he tried to suppress laughter. "The lace shop ladies? Explain."

"My do-or-die regulars. These are the serious collectors who come in every other week to brainstorm about stitch problems. Speaking of problems, the list of physical evidence in your file said there was a nail tip found at the crime scene, but the police assumed it belonged to Rayna, even though her acrylic nails were intact. Why did the police assume this?"

Jake thought for a minute. "Rayna wore fake nails all the time. No one would question it."

"Maybe a man wouldn't question it," Holly said.

"Say what?"

"I'm curious to know if there were any other nails in Rayna's house that matched the fake one found on her floor near her body."

Jake started to pace, stunned that he'd missed something so obvious. "How the hell should I know?"

"Maybe you ought to find out."

Jake had never considered the possibility that a woman might have killed Rayna. "What made you think of her nails, Holly?"

"It's something I noticed when I read your case file. It just seems weird that only one nail was found. Also, the color of the nail doesn't fit my image of Rayna."

"I don't follow. The nail could belong to anybody," Jake said.

"I really don't think so. If the nail belonged to Rayna, she'd have picked it up because it was part of a set. If it belonged to a friend, she'd have picked it up and returned it. Two friends might buy the same pair of nails for fun, but not three women, at least not at the same time. Then there's the color: lavender. Lavender doesn't go with everything."

Jake looked confused. "What's your theory?"

"Lavender doesn't go with everything. As a corporate exec, Rayna would need a color that went from daytime to nighttime with ease."

"And?"

"And so red would be a better choice than lavender," Holly explained. "Wine. Mocha. Taupe. Clear. Besides, the nail on the carpet had a butterfly on it. Rayna wouldn't wear designs unless it was for fun."

Jake's eyes sparked with interest. Her theory made sense, and he hoped it would help uncover the truth. The more time Jake spent with Holly, the more time he wanted to spend with her. "You're amazing."

"Thank you. Anyway, the nail on the carpet was one of those inexpensive nails you can buy as part of a set in Wal-Mart or somewhere like that. You know, in the section where you'll usually find the Sally Hansen nail products."

"Sally who?" She might as well have been speaking Russian for all Jake knew about acrylic nails.

"I'm serious, Jake."

"So am I. We're talking about murder."

"Well, it's a detail that's been bugging me. I mean, all we've done is skirt around Rayna's murder, over and over again. Nothing really changes, which means everything you need to solve the crime must be right in front of you."

Jake nodded his head slowly. "I'll get Kenneth to check into Dirk's whereabouts. It's possible he was the guy I caught spying."

"But wouldn't you recognize him?"

"Sometimes the best place to hide is in plain sight. I never expected to see Dirk in Guthrie. The more I think about it, the more I realize I might be right. Even though we were both suspects, neither of us believed the other did it."

"Hopefully Kenneth can get an answer for us tomorrow."

"Yeah. I'd also be interested to know if that nail has a print on it."

"That's good, Jake. Really good."

There was so much he liked about her, the casual way she regarded her own beauty, as if she had better things to worry about than the perfect curl in her hair. Holly wasn't reckless, she was resourceful, especially in her way of thinking. Most of all, she was kind, and that was salve to his soul.

By all accounts, he had it all, a successful manufacturing firm, a solid future, and money galore. But his zest for living had taken a downward spin, now that he was consumed by his need to avenge Rayna's murder. He was beginning to wonder how much about her was true, how much was illusion.

Had he seen only what he'd wanted to see? Had she been using him? There were more questions than answers cropping up since his moving to Guthrie, and he wanted answers.

He'd had to get away from Blue Springs in order to come up with a plan. Unwittingly, this had been an act of providence. Someone, Mr. Binoculars perhaps, had followed him from Blue Springs. And now, there was Holly.

Jake hadn't been looking for love when he met her. But thanks to her unflagging faith in all things good, he was quietly, steadily winning his battle between abiding by the law and taking matters into his own hands.

He wasn't sure what he'd do when he finally faced Rayna's killer, but one thing was certain, his slow-burning romance with Holly would affect his decision. He wanted her to be proud of him.

Seventeen

As much as she was involved in Jake's murder mystery, Holly still had a business to run. Having a staff added to her flexibility, but her being there, along with service and merchandise, is what kept her front door busy. Unlike Jake, she couldn't afford to take a long sabbatical. She was a small-shopkeeper and he ran a national corporation.

One thing she looked forward to each day was opening and closing the lace shop herself. In this way, she was able to check inventory, dust and tidy displays, and start the coffee.

Thanks to Daisy, she had become addicted to Seattle's Best coffee. However, unlike Daisy, Holly only drank coffee in the morning. Daisy practically mainlined it. Today was an exception. Today Holly had been pouring from the pot since she'd arrived, which meant she'd be wired for the rest of the night.

Because the shop was tiny, Holly didn't make a big deal about serving coffee. But she allowed customers to drink from her pot upon request. She'd discovered early on that coffee didn't go well with browsing in a fabric shop, as spills sometimes spelled disaster. But her regulars loved a good cup of coffee now and then, and she enjoyed supplying one.

Satisfied, Holly surveyed the contents of her store. Lace was much like the best of romances—delicate yet durable, distinctive yet ordinary, easy to treasure, and hard to hide when it was beautiful.

Her restoration clients did mostly repair work, on collars of old shirts, edging on lingerie, holes in dainty curtains, doilies, or bedding. One woman was restoring a Victorian lace canopy for her first granddaughter, and had turned her friends onto Yesterday Is Here Today.

Daisy arrived toward the end of the afternoon, her face beaming. "Kenneth says the man you and Jake chased at the country club drove off in a car registered to Dirk Adams."

"Rayna's business partner."

"Yep."

"We're finally getting somewhere," Holly said.

"Thank God."

"Want some coffee?" Holly asked. "It's on the old side, and a little dark, but you like it like that."

"Half a cup and keep it black," Daisy said. "Thanks."

"Cutting back?" Holly asked, a little surprised at her friend's request for only half a cup. Daisy had been drinking coffee by the gallon for years.

Daisy grimaced. "My poor body hit a caffeine overload last week. I've been drinking less coffee and sugar."

"Why don't you try decaf?"

Daisy shuddered. "I tried decaf yesterday and thought I'd croak. Half a cup straight up is better than two cups of decaf, let me tell you."

Another customer came in, then two more. While Holly waited on them, Daisy manned the cash register, something the two friends did for each other whenever things got busy.

After the customers left, Holly dished up the gossip her friend had been patiently waiting to hear. "Spud is a problem."

Daisy set aside her cup after draining the last drop of coffee. "It's been killing me not to bring it up."

"I can't believe how possessive he's been acting."

Daisy kicked off her rubber gardening clogs. Once again, she'd forgotten to exchange her clogs for regular sandals before she left work. It was a coincidence she wore a green shirt that matched the shoes. "Not exactly the big brother kind of possessive, I gather."

"I wish it were that simple," Holly said. "I think he wants Jake to be guilty of something. Daisy, he was terrible."

"Why are you so surprised Spud is jealous? He's always cared about you."

Holly sighed. "I don't think of him in a romantic way, and we've never discussed it. Spud was sitting in the driveway in his squad car when I left the house this morning. He looked like he wanted to punch Jake for staying the night."

Jake chose that moment to walk through the door. He was handsome in a dark blue shirt with matching khaki pants, and dark loafers with tassels.

"Ladies," he said, as his eyes devoured Holly. She was dressed in red from lips to toenails. She was a little chili pepper all right, his pepper.

"Hey, Jake," Daisy said, as she gave him a quick peck on the cheek. "Kenneth expects word back any minute about the fingerprint you asked him to look into. He'll probably be calling you soon."

She gave Holly a hug. "I'll call you tonight."

"Sounds good. Thanks for helping with the register."

Jake's gray eyes swept over the lace shop. He'd just

figured out what was wrong. "Where's your afternoon clerk?"

Holly tried to be nonchalant. She wasn't supposed to be alone when Jake couldn't be with her. "She had to take her daughter to the doctor. No big deal."

Before he could argue, she changed the subject. "I heard Dirk's in town."

"Yes," Jake said. "The police are looking for him."

"Good."

"When you look at me like that," he said, "I feel as if bricks have been lifted off my shoulders."

She couldn't think of a thing to say, so she slid off her stool and wrapped her arms around him, holding him as tight as she could. He was hard as stone, and equally as tough in his commitment to find Rayna's killer. She could only imagine how deeply he'd love the woman he chose as his own.

"Come on," he said. "Maybe we can make it back to your house without getting stopped by your friends. After I dropped you off this morning, a farmer stared at me as if he wanted to shoot me. He probably figures I'm guilty until proven innocent."

"Will you flip the sign while I empty the cash register?"

Just as Jake put his hand on the sign, several regulars pushed their way inside. He wanted to groan. "Hello," he said.

Holly looked up. "Y'all know good and well we meet on Tuesday night. This is not Tuesday."

"We're not here for that and you know it," Cinnamon Hartfeld said. She looked plump and pampered, which she was.

No-nonsense Zenith eyed Jake with the cool eye of a woman who knew a thing or two about wild, wayward men who might be criminals. "So," she said, "this is the hottie you've been playing hide-and-seek with."

"Jake Fishbone," he said, "at your service."

Holly put the case from the register in her purse. "You guys are embarrassing me."

Cinnamon laughed. "Quit lyin'. Nothing embarrasses you."

The very matronly Miss Myrtle adjusted her pageboy wig and motioned Jake to the long worktable in the rear of the shop. "May as well sit down, fella. Ain't none of us going anywhere any time soon."

Holly tried to intervene. These women weren't in a hurry to go anywhere, but she needed some privacy for her own sake. Jake could take care of himself. These women knew where most of her hangouts were. They would track her to hell and back. She just wished they'd had better timing. "I'm closed," she said. "Closed. Please read the sign."

Miss Tilly added her two cents. Except for the pageboy wig, she and Miss Myrtle might have been sisters. Instead, the women were sisters-in-law who had married brothers, both of whom were now deceased. "Sign says you're open, Holly."

Holly stopped arguing. Besides Cinnamon, Zenith, Missy Tilly, and Miss Myrtle, she normally had six to eight people every week in the Tuesday group. She was lucky only these four showed up. "Okay, you guys. What's up?"

Cinnamon's smile was contagious. "Basically, we wanna help."

"Good," Jake said. "The more people paying attention to what's going on, the more anything suspicious will be noticed."

Zenith leaned forward. "There's some woman running around town asking questions about Holly. She pretended to be interested in buying some lace. But when I gave her directions to the shop, she acted like she didn't want to hear that part. She wanted to know how long Holly had lived here. How long she'd been in business. Junk like that."

Holly was stunned. She opened her mouth to speak, but couldn't. Only an out-of-towner would think such questions would go unnoticed. Families and friends knew each other for generations in Guthrie. Without realizing it, the stranger had stood out. "Well," she finally said.

"Zenith told Spud," Cinnamon added. "Spud gave a description of the woman to the police here and to Kenneth, who said he was gonna run it by you and the Blue Springs police."

"When did all this happen?" Jake asked.

"About an hour ago," Cinnamon said. "It's why we came over. We figured it would be faster to tell you two in person than it would be to wait for Spud and Kenneth to finish telling the cops or whoever it is they need to tell."

Holly hardly knew what to say. "Thank you."

"You're welcome," the four women chimed in at once.

They each gave Holly a hug on their way out. Their mission had been accomplished; plus they'd been able to see Jake with Holly. It was clear, at least to them, that he adored her. They wanted to see for themselves that she wasn't making an idiot out of herself. He was Daisy's cousin, yes, but even cousins weren't always the best references.

Spud appeared, greeting the ladies, escorting Miss Myrtle and Miss Tilly to Miss Tilly's Buick Century.

After they left, he turned to Holly. "Maybe we ought to go back inside the shop. We need to talk."

"Can't we just drive over to my place and talk?" Holly asked.

"There's a storm coming," Spud said. "Sounds like it might get nasty. Thunder, lightning, high winds. The works."

Inside the shop, Holly turned on the rear lights to help them see where they were going in the semidark. Cinnamon Hartfeld was waiting for them. Nobody, Jake included, noticed her slip in. Her presense revealed how easily Holly and Jake could be targeted.

Holly shook her head. "Just keep quiet about whatever you hear, okay?"

Spud interrupted. "We're discussing a murder case, Cinnamon."

"Everybody who knows Holly knows you're discussing Rayna's murder."

Spud looked at Cinnamon as if he'd just noticed she was gorgeous. Cinnamon batted her lashes. They all sat down.

Spud began talking just as the thunder roared outside. His radio squawked, but nothing pressing drew him away. "There's been another break in the investigation."

"Go on," Jake said.

"The acrylic nail had a fingerprint on it," Spud said. "It belonged to a woman named Tina Nolan."

"My ex-secretary."

"Right."

Jake was silent a moment, as more thunder boomed above the shop. The sky was unnaturally dark, and rain splashed against the windows. "Where is Tina?"

"Nobody knows," Spud said. "Blue Springs police

found a wall in her bedroom loaded with shots of you, Jake."

More thunder boomed outside.

Cinnamon snuggled up next to Spud. Her breast pressed against his arm. "Gosh," she said. "Holly really is in trouble."

Almost reflexively, Spud put an arm around Cinnamon's shoulders, but his eyes were on Jake. "It ain't possible to keep you totally protected all day and night, even though that's what the police round here are trying to do. Be prepared for anything, Fishbone. That includes everything and nothing."

Jake nodded. The storm would keep Spud busy until it blew over, which from the sound of the wind and the rain wouldn't be very soon. Jake was Holly's best protection tonight.

"I hear you, Gurber," Jake said. "I'm not letting Holly out of my sight."

Eighteen

In fifteen minutes, Jake and Holly were back at her place. It was 7:00 P.M. A severe thunderstorm was wreaking havoc in the city of Guthrie. Lightning etched spectacular images against the unnaturally dark sky as thunder rattled the dishes and wind shook the windows.

Normally, Holly enjoyed nights like this. Her only worry was the threat of a tornado. It was the time of year when funnel clouds touched down with destructive results. Her television was set on *News 9,* which tracked the storm that might send her to the cellar for safety at a moment's notice. For now, there was just a tornado watch in the Guthrie area.

After taking a short shower, Holly dressed in a soft pair of floral-print pants and a gauzy spring top. Her mission now was to make dinner for two. While Jake kept an eye on the news, she removed a stainless steel pot from one of the kitchen cupboards, filled it with water, and turned the burner on so the water would boil. She had decided on fettuccine Alfredo, a quick and easy dish that went great with salad, bread, and wine, which was about all she had on hand.

Trying to avoid thinking about any problems, Holly concentrated on not overcooking the fettuccine. She chopped several cloves of garlic, and three bunches of green onion, which she sautéed in a skillet of melted butter.

She next prepared the salad, a packaged spinach mix, to which she added slices of cucumber, green onion, olives, and broken bits of bacon. She chopped two of the boiled eggs she kept on hand and added shredded cheese.

She drained the noodles and returned them to the pot. She then added the garlic-onion-butter mixture along with heavy cream, seasoned salt, and pepper. She tossed in some dried parsley for taste, with some serious dashes of Parmesan cheese to give the fettuccine a bit more oomph.

The meal she prepared had been simple, would look great on her Royal Copenhagen dinner plates, and would eliminate the need for dessert. They wouldn't be able to move once they were done eating.

After the tornado watch was over, Jake turned off the television set, switched on the answering machine, and helped Holly put the finishing touches on the meal. They were both quiet, each appreciating the other in what had turned out to be an extremely intimate and private evening. They were a couple on the brink of a committed, loving relationship. Jake would always remember this night.

The passing of the tornado watch made it feel as if they were sheltered from harm. The simple domestic chores they shared were a source of grounding, centering them. The wood table was covered in lace, something soft and very old. Jake dimmed the lights, lit burgundy-colored candles, and laid a rose by her plate. He'd stolen the flower from a bush in her front yard.

The overall effect of the setting was calming, simple,

and tasteful. The dining room was an open area just off the living room. Nothing was muted here, as patterns and colors tumbled together. The lace was used to accent the decor and went along with the pressed-back chairs, which were rustic and painted a dark hunter green to match the rug beneath the table.

Jake wasn't surprised to realize that he didn't want to leave. In Guthrie, there was opportunity. He could shift his business headquarters here, or telecommute. Most important, Holly was here. He couldn't imagine living the rest of his life without her.

As he loaded the CD player with soft dinner music, he thought about how he might repay some of the kindness she'd shown him. He could bring her backyard to life with birds by building an urban habitat, as she had brought him to life by rekindling his creativity in his work. His creativity rekindled his passion, which in turn had led him to love. Unwilling to commit without closure on Rayna, he could show his appreciation for her patience.

There were several foundation shrubs and trees on Holly's lot, but nothing really commandeered a second look, except for her single stunning rosebush. A birdbath would complement her roses, a yellow-orange-red bush in dire need of a hard pruning.

He'd mowed her lawn while she worked, weed-whacked her fencing and around her porch steps without realizing her regular clerk was off to care for a sick child. Holly had been alone, unguarded, in an attempt to return to her normal life. Daisy must have heard she was alone, because she'd abandoned her own business to sit and visit with her friend. As he listened to the music play, Jake realized he wanted to be the only one Holly turned to for help.

While Jake fantasized about a future with Holly, she was doing the same thing about him. In the kitchen, she wiped down the countertops and loaded a few items in the dishwasher, her only modern addition other than updated electrical wiring. Her kitchen was old, the house itself a throwback to the early 1930s.

She had no idea when she'd ever get the money to refurbish the kitchen properly, but she'd painted the cupboards a butter yellow, and had found ceramic knobs that were white with blue and yellow flowers. The floors were paved in brick, with decorated anti-fatigue mats on the floor next to the sink and stove.

She'd hung copper pots and pans from the ceiling. Instead of a small dinette table, she'd opted for a huge center island, one with distressed, beaded boards that she'd painted an off-white. She ate most of her meals here, whether she had company or not, but not tonight. Tonight was special.

Humming to herself, Holly set the meal on the table while Jake took his turn in the shower. He'd promised to be ready within the next ten minutes. Using the time to tidy herself up, she was surprised to hear the doorbell ring.

She hurried to answer the summons, thinking that perhaps it was Spud with good news. Spoiled by her easygoing lifestyle, and assuming she knew who was at the door, Holly didn't think twice about throwing it open.

In the wind-whipped rain, a woman stood there, her hair a damp cascade down her back, a gun in her hand, lightning flashing behind her. From inside the house, eighties music from Luther Vandross played in the background.

Too late, Holly recognized her fatal mistake. Even

in this small, cozy town, bad things happened to good people. She tried to slam the door shut, but the woman pointed the weapon at her.

The gun was a Smith and Wesson third-generation semiautomatic pistol, and the woman handled the gun as if she knew how to use it. It had three levels of safety: on the firing pin, the safety catch, and the magazine. All the safeties were off.

The woman crossed the threshold, kicked the door closed with the heel of her New Balance sneaker, and motioned for Holly to step back, which she did without argument. Her throat was too tight for her to speak.

"Where's Jake?" the stranger softly demanded.

The laundry room door banged shut in the back of the house. Barefoot and smelling good, Jake appeared in the living room. He was dressed in jeans and a chambray shirt. "Tina?" he said. "Tina Nolan?"

"Sit down, folks," the woman in hot pink said, her nylon running suit soaked with rain. "Let's talk."

Holly sat. She'd been on her p's and q's all day, only to wind up letting her guard down at the wrong time. What a way to end her crime story with Jake. She couldn't believe she'd opened the front door without asking who rang the bell. Had it only been yesterday she was calling Spud and Jake morons? She was the stupid one.

Jake refused to sit down. While he'd been daydreaming about a future with Holly, Tina Nolan had been casing the joint.

Tina's laugh was wicked. She was near the end of her master plan. An image consultant in Blue Springs, she'd already invented a fresh persona for herself. She had plane tickets in another name and she was headed to another country—as soon as she dispensed with the lovebirds.

"I said, sit down, Jake. Now."

Holly didn't care for the grit in the stranger's tone. "Jake," she called from the sofa, "maybe you ought to do what she says."

Jake still didn't move. Tina was small. He bet he could take her out with one tackle. That was the easy part. The crazy part was whether or not Tina would get a shot off before he reached her.

Holly willed him not to lose his cool now. He'd been levelheaded up to this point, but he was angry enough now to do something dangerous. This only made Tina's gun more deadly. She might be pushed into using it in order to defend herself.

Holly wrapped her arms around her chest, but found little comfort. If Jake Fishbone was shot to death in this house, she'd get a taste of the grief he'd been dealing with full-time over his friend Rayna.

She'd be guilty of letting his killer waltz into the house with an open invitation. There would be no jimmy marks on the door frame, no broken windows to show forced entry. Holly had been warned and warned again to be careful, but she hadn't listened, not really.

Why hadn't she been more careful? Why hadn't she believed that his keeping her close was more than paranoia, it was a necessity? Where was Spud Gurber, for crying out loud?

He was out patrolling the streets of Guthrie the way he was supposed to be doing, that's where he was. He'd trusted Jake to protect her. Jake had trusted her not to take any chances, and she, blast her own careless hide, had let a killer into the house.

Jake sat down beside Holly, but he didn't look

scared. He looked hell-bent on revenge. This frightened Holly more than Tina Nolan's gun did.

She knew what that gun could do, if it was in fact loaded, but she didn't know what to expect from Jake. He was a predatory presence in the living room, a huge angry man held in check by the threat of a single bullet.

"Why here?" he asked. "Why now?"

"Loose ends," Tina answered. "They've gotta go, gotta go."

Holly gasped. Was this woman crazy? Were they all doomed? *Yes,* her mind shouted. Yes, and she wouldn't be able to have her last meal. She and Jake would never solve the case and live happily ever after. Her shop would be ruined. Justice would not be served.

"Why'd you kill Rayna?" Jake asked.

Tina shrugged. "She stood in the way of our happiness. Simple as that."

With all the thunder, wind, and rain, Jake wasn't sure Holly's neighbors would notice if a gun went off. The harsh, intermittent sounds of the storm made great cover. It took every scrap of his control not to leap at Tina's throat. She'd selected a prime moment to make her move. He needed to be just as careful, just as ready when opportunity struck.

Unlike Holly, he was certain the gun was loaded. He recognized the effort it took for Tina to keep it steady in her hand. He spoke in a low, conversational tone that didn't match the suppressed violence in his eyes.

"What made you think we could make it, Tina?" Jake asked.

"You. It's why you asked me to join you for dinner with your friends."

"Those weren't my friends, they were potential

clients. You were my executive secretary. All we ever did was work," Jake said.

"We worked long, long hours sometimes, Jake. We ate takeout in the office sometimes."

"Those weren't dates," Jake said. "This is crazy."

"Rayna was the crazy one. She threatened to tell you about me."

"You aren't making any sense. None of this makes sense. Did you think I was going to turn to you after Rayna died, or something like that?" Jake asked.

"You should have turned to me," Tina said. "I was at the funeral."

Veins stood out in Jake's neck. "Where's Dirk Adams?" he asked.

"Dead."

"Why, Tina?" Jake asked. "Why'd you kill him?"

"He figured everything out."

Holly wanted to run. Jake was too calm. Tina was too calm. The storm was raging and the end of her world was at hand. Neighbors who might normally be sitting on the porch were inside because the weather was bad. They weren't going to be much help.

Holly didn't know any martial arts or basic self-defense. She'd never been in a catfight, let alone a gunfight. Nobody won when it came to guns, and this Tina Nolan had already committed murder twice.

Jake hadn't known what the murderer looked like, but he'd known it was someone close to the victim. He hadn't known where the murderer lived, but he'd drawn the killer to him. Now, because of his perseverance, he'd been able to lay hands upon her.

The phone rang.

Startled, Tina jumped.

Jake lunged across the coffee table and knocked

her down, but Tina still managed to get a shot off. The bullet blasted a hole in the ceiling.

As dust and plaster crumbled to the floor, Daisy made a recording on the answering machine: "Holly? Are you there, girlfriend? Come on, pick up, will you? Police found a dead guy they think Jake might know. His name is Dirk Adams."

Within moments, police sirens were heard. The rain had slowed, but lightning still flashed. There was thunder, but only in the distance. Holly's neighbors had been listening after all. Two different sets of them had heard the gunshot and called the police. The unofficial neighborhood watch had been in full effect.

Shocked speechless once again, Holly watched in mounting amazement as Jake snatched a length of lace off the back of the couch and used it to tie Tina's wrists. In the entire history of lace, she'd bet money it had never been used this way before.

Spud stormed through the front door, fellow police officers in tow. There were neighbors on the lawn with crowbars. Someone had called Cinnamon and Zenith, who nearly crashed their cars in their haste to save Holly. Miss Tilly lived across the street and all the lights were on at her house. She was making coffee for the various rescue squads, Seattle's Best coffee from D.G.'s.

Tomorrow, Yesterday Is Here Today would be booming.

Glad Kenneth had arrived and was taking charge of the crowd, Jake tore away from the press of investigators in order to be with Holly.

"Hey," he said, "you okay?"

She found her voice. "Just hold me, Jake. Hold me tight."

He crushed her in his arms. Justice had been

served and he was a free man. He could now love Holly the way she deserved, with all his heart, his body, his soul. "Don't worry, sweetheart. I'm not going anywhere."

Nineteen

The next day

Jake and Spud were in another standoff. Their legs were braced wide, their arms akimbo. "You can back off now, Gurber," Jake said. "I've got things under control here."

"I want to see her," Spud said.

Holly came to the door. "I've got to be one of the luckiest women in town," she said. "Let him in, Jake."

They went to the kitchen, where Holly poured soft drinks. She'd hoped the two would find a way to at least be civil, but she wasn't sure it was going to be possible.

"I appreciate all you've done, Spud," she said. "But I love Jake. He makes me happy, so you're going to have to get that through your head."

Spud wasn't ready to let go of his dream to be with Holly. "I guess I always thought we'd be good together," he said. "I just wish I hadn't waited so long to tell you."

"My answer would have been the same no matter when you talked to me," Holly said. "You're a great friend, Spud, but I've never thought of us as a couple."

"Why did you go on that date with me, then?"

"Because you're fun," Holly said. "You always make me laugh."

The kitchen was thick with tension.

"What she wants is what I want," Spud said grudgingly to Jake. "But if you hurt her, Fishbone, I'll kick your butt."

"I hear you," Jake said. He didn't like any part of this conversation and it showed in his face.

Holly placed a calming hand on each of them. "Daisy did some matchmaking for me, Spud. I'm gonna do the same for you."

Spud clamped his teeth down on the toothpick in his mouth. A muscle worked in his jaw. One glance at Jake and the men were suddenly on the same side—two men against a matchmaking woman.

"Let it go, Holly," Jake said.

Holly laughed softly. "You guys carry on as if I'm a bone between you. I've got a stake in your argument. I don't see why we all can't be happy."

Jake and Spud looked at her, then turned to look at each other. "Holly," they said in unison.

"I'm serious," Holly said. "Spud, do you realize that Cinnamon Hartfeld is nuts about you?"

Spud was startled. "How do you know this?" he asked.

"Anyone paying attention can see it," Holly said. "Why else do you think she barged into the lace shop last night after all the other ladies had gone home? She came to see you. Sometimes the best things in life are right in your own backyard."

Jake made a grunting noise. "Holly's right," he said, thinking about Rayna being in love with him, only he'd been too blind to notice. "At least give the idea a chance."

Spud looked at Jake. "I'll back off," he said. "But I'll be around if Holly ever needs me."

"That's nice to know," Jake said, offering his hand to shake. "At least we both want the same thing, which is to make Holly happy."

"I've got to hand it to you, Fishbone, for not buckling under the pressure of that murder case," Spud said. "I respect you for that."

"And I appreciate the way you looked after Holly, even though you knew I didn't like it. I guess there really isn't any more reason to fight about who gets the girl."

Spud got up to leave. "No," he said, "there isn't."

Jake drew her into his arms as soon as Spud left. "Glad that's over with," he said. "If we weren't busy fighting over you, we could probably be friends."

Holly pressed her face against Jake's chest, loving the feel of him. "I think he likes you too, only he wishes he didn't. I'm sure it'll all work out eventually."

Jake got down on one knee, holding Holly's hands with his own. "I love you," he said. "I want you to be my wife."

Holly's eyes glistened with unshed tears. She hadn't been looking for a hero, but she'd found one in Jake. "Hmm," she said. "Holly Fishbone. I can't wait to tell the girls."

Jake tumbled her gently to her knees, so that they faced each other. "I promise never to take you for granted, Holly."

"And I promise that you'll never be bored."

Jake was taken aback. "What do you mean?"

"You still haven't met the rest of the family."

Someone knocked on the door.

"And here's one of them now."

"Who?" Jake asked.

"William."

"How do you know it's him?"

"It's the way he knocks. Growing up, my brothers had a clubhouse in the backyard. Each brother had a secret knock. I learned all their knocks so I could trick them into letting me in. Now, the knocking is done jokingly. William is trying to be discreet by letting me know he's here. Spud probably told him the case is solved."

"Spud?"

"Yep. William and Spud have been friends a lot longer than me and Holly."

Jake groaned. "No wonder Spud was so aggressive."

Holly winked. "He was spying for William."

"You're right," Jake said, as he rubbed his thumb over her bottom lip. "I'll never be bored, but guess what?"

"What?"

"You haven't met my family, either."

As Jake and Holly brought William up to speed about the solved murder case, they realized how much their lives had changed since they met.

Jake was the kind of man who recognized a good woman when he saw her. Holly was this kind of woman. Feminine and emotionally tough, she hadn't been afraid to risk her life to save him, a stranger. She had saved him from becoming a bitter man.

He'd always thought Rayna Holdenbrook was the only woman who would ever understand him. She had known that in order to be close to him, she had to be second to his career. In his selfish need to succeed in business, he'd failed to notice that whatever she did for him had been done because she loved him.

Epilogue

Tina Nolan admitted her guilt to the various criminal charges against her and provided reasons for her actions. Some of her reasons made sense, others did not.

Police found a set of acrylic nails matching the one found at Rayna's crime scene. The nail had been the single most important clue that led investigators to break the case.

Jake's personal case file was in the hands of the Blue Springs police, who had found a similar setup in Dirk's briefcase. Both men had committed themselves to discovering the truth.

Jake's name was cleared. His reputation in Blue Springs, Arkansas, remained tainted, but his true friends were still his friends.

After some serious wrangling with Guthrie city officials, Jake found a business site large enough to accommodate his headquarters. Within a year, he expected the facility to be built from the ground up, and fully functioning. For now, his manufacturing facility remained in Blue Springs. His parents ran that part of the business.

With Jake's help, Holly expanded her own business. His marketing staff designed a Web site for her, which increased her customer base dramatically. Yesterday Is

Here Today was nationwide, with growing contacts in the international market. Going international increased Holly's access to museum-quality lace pieces, which were in demand by serious collectors.

Now when he thought about Rayna's murder, Jake felt as if justice had been served. The truth about who had killed her and why she was killed was public knowledge. It was sad that it took the death of a close friend to make him realize how much he had taken his life for granted. He no longer felt guilty about not being there to save Rayna, but he would always miss her.

In his dreams, Jake saw her smiling. Sometimes, he heard her laugh. He liked to believe that the healing had begun. He owed much of this to Holly, who was very much alive. Her optimism had been uplifting from the moment they first met. She was the reason he planned to stay in Guthrie.

With a population of ten thousand, Guthrie was the perfect place to expand the feed side of Jake's business. He planned to buy enough acreage locally to grow and process his own raw materials.

Holly was the glue that made his new career goal hang together. Their friends Daisy and Kenneth Gunn were extremely supportive. They helped Jake make solid business connections locally, referring him to the plumbers, electricians, and contractors he needed to get the warehouse into shape. It felt good to be able to work again.

Holly helped Jake understand the difference between working hard and being a workaholic. He worked twelve-hour days getting his new business venture off the ground. But evenings and weekends were spent with Holly.

Together, they browsed the shops in downtown

Guthrie. Holly took him to the various museums and art galleries. They furnished his house with tables and chairs from Elk's Alley, with picture frames and candleholders from Near and Far. Holly made a housewarming gift of hundred-year-old lace for his guest bedroom.

Holly was thankful she'd taken a chance on Jake. She'd discovered that his heart was big and giving now that his reputation had been restored. She sometimes pinched herself to make sure she wasn't dreaming.

He was generous with his love, showering her with kisses, gifts of flowers, and a steady supply of ice cream from Brahm's. She liked the way he threw himself into their relationship, as if he never wanted her to forget how much he appreciated her. There was nothing high maintenance about him. He was a green-light man all the way.

Dear Readers:

As an Arabesque author, I thank you for your support over the years. It feels as if a lifetime has come and gone, where I find myself stiff and gray, but wiser than when *Delicious* first sold. As always, I thank you for keeping up with my body of work. Often it is the reader who inspires the writer to keep facing that blank computer screen.

I wish you and your families the best. As for me, the best is here in my own backyard. I hope this is the same for you.

Warm regards,

Shelby

If you enjoyed this novel,
please read the other titles
in this series—*Simply Wonderful*
and *Simply Marvelous*.

Turn the page for a preview of *Simply Marvelous* . . .

One

Saturday afternoon,
first week of June

When Kenneth Gunn stepped off the airplane, he had no idea he was stepping into a drama-filled week. A private detective in Wichita, Kansas, he'd made plans for a romantic visit with his girlfriend, Daisy Rogers, a retail nursery and garden shop owner in Guthrie, Oklahoma. The only strain in their relationship was the long traveling distance between them. It meant they couldn't see each other every day the way they wanted to, which made their time together that much sweeter.

On this occasion, Kenneth was flying in from a business trip in Dallas where he'd just finished solving a missing persons case, one that had ended on a positive note; he'd been able to reunite a runaway teen with his family. Kenneth looked forward to some quality downtime with Daisy, his way of regrouping between cases.

In order to get to Guthrie, he'd flown from Dallas on a commuter airplane to the Will Rogers Airport in Oklahoma City. From this point, he needed a car to get from Oklahoma City to Guthrie, which he preferred so that he'd have his own wheels during his brief holiday. However, on this trip, Daisy had opted to pick him up in her full-size Chevy truck. Kenneth had never dated a woman who owned a truck before, and he couldn't imagine Daisy driving anything different.

Daisy. The excitement of seeing her again made Kenneth forget that the small airplane had been too hot and that a seven-month-old baby girl aboard had cried the whole way. He'd found himself eyeing the small brown baby and wondering if he'd ever have one of his own. If he did, he'd want a girl, one who looked just like Daisy.

Daisy. Kenneth wondered if she'd pick him up wearing a next-to-nothing dress or her usual jeans, T-shirt, and green rubber gardening clogs. She looked good in everything or nothing at all, his favorite way to see her whenever they were alone together. Whatever she wore, she was never self-conscious, and he liked the way she was so relaxed with herself. She was pretty without primping and he liked this, too.

Dressed all in black, Kenneth strode through the quiet, makeshift tunnel from the plane to the lobby and straight into Daisy's arms. She felt soft and warm and cuddly. He was hard in an instant. "Baby," he said low in her ear, "it's been six weeks too long."

They had talked on the phone as often as they could, but Kenneth's schedule wasn't predictable and they often missed each other, an absence they tried to remedy by talking for hours at a stretch, like teenagers in love, oblivious of the passage of time, so that hours seemed like minutes, and days were like hours.

Kenneth knew that this visit to see Daisy would feel shorter than a full seven days. Though intense, his visits seldom lasted long enough for him to feel restless for his normal routine in Wichita. He never felt as good upon leaving her home in Guthrie as he did upon arriving. Once he left, he was very conscious of time.

Hours felt like days and days were months that stretched forever until the next moment they could be together again. Without Daisy, Kenneth felt lonely. He hated feeling lonely, and for a brief moment, his dark eyes reflected that unhappy thought.

Daisy saw the moment and responded to it playfully. She placed a chaste kiss on his lips, but the look in her eyes told him a different, quite provocative story, one that revealed all the subtle details of her desires.

She, too, had been lonely, a woman keenly aware of the late hours of night when the only thing warm to hold on to tight was the pillow beside her in a bed so big, it dominated the bedroom they would soon share together.

Not a woman who restrained her feelings, Daisy stripped him stark naked with her eyes in two seconds flat. Her body radiated with anticipation. She said, "Let's skip dinner." She was a tease who knew how to please.

Kenneth's excitement jumped up a notch. He forced himself to walk and not run to her waiting vehicle. He was too old and too dignified to show the casual onlookers around them in the airport how very hot and horny he was at just the sight of the woman who refused to wear his engagement ring. He chose to grin like a fool instead, a reflection of the jittery feeling in the pit of his stomach, a feeling that reminded him he'd missed breakfast that morning in his haste to make it to the airport on time to catch his flight from Dallas.

All negativity was suspended whenever Kenneth came together with Daisy, suspended in the comfortable way that happens between people who truly enjoy each other's company and rarely run out of words to say. He spoke without thinking first, a rare treat in his line of work. On this day, at this time, all his emotions were unguarded, his happiness as open and kind as the woman whose spirit lifted his soul. "Good thing you're closed tomorrow," he said.

Daisy gave his arm a playful squeeze. His skin felt tight, the muscles rippling beneath her fingers. *Ooh,* she thought. *Ooh.* Instead of telling him flat out what she was thinking, she said a little breathlessly, "Why?"

He laughed as if the sun were shining straight into his heart, a light that was bold and bright and beautiful. Being with Daisy made him feel as if he were breathing cool mountain air. His words came out in a low growl. "We're gonna be up all night."

She leered at him. "Promise?"

"Promise."

Her laugh, delicious and sexy, sent ripples of desire along the insides of his heavy thighs. "You make me forget it's storming outside," he said.

"Oh, yeah?" she quizzed, her silky lashes fluttering ridiculously. She felt as if her very skin was energized by Kenneth's presence.

"Yeah," he said. "I was probably the one person on the plane only half distracted by the air turbulence we had just before landing. If my flight had been later, I probably would have been delayed. Like I said, six weeks is too long between visits. I felt every second."

She spiked her voice with a come-hither note. "More reason to play hide-and-seek under the covers."

He threw an arm around her and squeezed gently.

In his mind, he pictured the ebony-colored mole beneath the palm he now used to cup her shoulder bone. She had several lovely flat moles scattered over her body, but this particular mole was his favorite.

It was his spot because when he played connect the dots with his kisses, he started with the mole on her right shoulder and worked his way to the mole on her left ankle. He said, "I love the way you speak your mind."

She squeezed him back. "I love you, too, but it's not your mind I'm thinking about right now."

He laughed with gusto. "Same here. It's why I packed only the bag I'm holding." He lifted the leather duffel in order to show her.

"No need to stop at baggage claim?"

"Nope."

Smiling, she pulled him down so she could whisper in his ear, "I like it when you talk dirty."

He dropped his hand from her shoulder in order to lock their fingers together. Her hand felt strong and soft at the same time. "Baby, you ain't heard nothin' yet."

With his bag in the rear seat of Daisy's extended-cab truck, freshly detailed by Brett's Auto Detailing in Guthrie, Kenneth was glad she tossed him the keys so he could drive. Driving would keep his hands and his mind occupied during the forty-minute commute from the city to Daisy's home in Guthrie, the quaint Victorian-style town that suited her personality so perfectly.

Guthrie suited Daisy because, like her, the small city welcomed the eccentric as well as it accepted the varied social classes that were the cornerstones of its character, a place where the descendants of the original wealthy were still called founding fathers. In Daisy's hometown the farmers and ranchers were often land rich and cash poor; the elderly managed to live in their own homes through their eighties and nineties, while the young left Guthrie to work in Stillwater, Norman, Edmond, and Oklahoma City. There was little industry in Guthrie, something Kenneth felt hurt its economy. He hoped this would soon change.

While many businesses in Guthrie were successful because they focused on tourist trade, Daisy's Rose Nursery and Garden Shop was successful because Daisy was a true hometown girl. She was born and raised in Guthrie, was respected and well liked in the close-knit community, and when she'd opened her doors for business, the locals had flocked to her garden center in numbers so steady that she'd opened in the financial black and stayed in the black.

She stayed in the black because she focused on service and quality merchandise. Whenever possible, she offered expert gardening tips to her customers and concentrated her business on flowers that thrived in Oklahoma weather and flourished in the red, heavy clay soil that dominated Guthrie land, Logan County land.

Kenneth recognized that the same care and dedication Daisy brought to her business, she brought to their relationship. She spread praise like fertilizer, hope like water, and whenever a problem surfaced between them, she tackled it the way she tackled challenges in her gardens—by examining them objectively and then ridding herself of them quickly and systematically until only the beauty, or at least the promise of beauty, reigned once again. He admired her tenacity, her willingness to go the extra mile. It was a trait they shared.

In turn, Daisy was content to rest in the seat beside Kenneth. She was usually closed on Sundays, but she often did a spot check of the gardens, just to make sure everything was okay. Sometimes unwanted birds or small critters made their way into the nursery and she liked to keep caterpillars from eating the leaves of flowers designated for sale. In this way, she kept her wares in optimum condition.

She was glad she had made no plans to tend the garden shop the following day so that she could enjoy two full nights alone with her love before she returned to her regular daily routine of running her business. Daisy's Rose Nursery and Garden Shop. Just seeing the hand-lettered sign made her proud.

Located on South Division in Guthrie, U.S. Highway 77, the garden shop served as Daisy's oasis, a place that was neutral because it brought together people from all age groups and walks of life, from young stay-at-home mothers to weekend gardeners to retirees. She rarely felt her job was a burden. Instead, she thrived in her chosen profession.

In this regard, Daisy's work complemented Kenneth's work, which also dealt with people from all age groups and walks of life. A private investigator, he specialized in missing persons cases, although he often gathered information for insurance companies or provided security background checks for employers, dignitaries, athletes, and entertainers.

Very little of his work was hazardous, most of it involving elementary deduction, commonsense reasoning, and attention to detail. On the odd occasion he needed extra help, he hired it and billed the client.

Daisy operated on a similar level. She hired extra hands when needed, mostly during peak seasons.

In the companionable silence of the truck, Kenneth felt an odd sense of peace when he crossed from Oklahoma County into Logan County, where Daisy lived. He registered the bumpy road, and the feel of Daisy beside him, her hand resting suggestively near the apex of his thighs, the tip of her index finger caressing him in a slow absentminded type of rhythm.

Because she trusted him behind the wheel, she was able to relax, her head resting against the passenger seat, her eyes closed as she listened to George Benson playing on the stereo. The song they listened to was called "I Just Wanna Hang Around You" and the words the aging jazz guitar player sang were just right.

Inside the truck's cab, the smooth jazz between them, it was easy to imagine their hearts beating as one, that their minds were filled with thoughts of each other. The mood spelled anticipation, a feeling shared by both.

Kenneth wished they could stay together in Daisy's house until they ran out of food and other necessities. Thinking about her responsibilities, he asked, "What exactly will you be doing for this show you're having?" She had a regular workweek scheduled, in addition to running her first garden show.

She sighed, as if she was reluctant to break her restful silence with talk about her job. Still, she understood why he asked. He was right to ask. She believed communication was nine-tenths of a long and satisfying relationship. They needed to be clear on how much playtime could be carved from her work schedule. The spring and summer seasons were her busiest times of year and it was never easy for her to gain free time. This week was an impossible one for Daisy.

She said, "First of all, this show is strictly for amateurs. We'll be focusing on living plants. We'll have judges and teachers of miniclasses in horticulture as well as news media coverage. It's a big deal, bigger than I first expected." It had snowballed from the idea phase to its final execution, and props still had to be made. Thinking of everything she had left to do before the event made her tense, her earlier euphoria quickly disappearing.

"Will there be any cosponsors?" Kenneth asked. He was surprised at how involved and serious the show had turned out to be. It sounded as if it would be a major event, and for the first time, he realized that he hadn't really been listening when she'd updated him on her plans prior to this visit. He'd been caught up in his missing persons case.

He wanted to be supportive but he actually wished Daisy had nothing so specific planned for the week. He had known she would be busy, but not as busy as it now sounded as if she would be. He supposed he should be grateful that she'd made the time to pick him up from the airport at all. She had to be tired from planning and organizing the flower show while running the garden shop full-time. No longer kicked back with her eyes closed, she was staring out the window.

Daisy was silent because she was thinking. She'd noted the shift in Kenneth's attitude, from being slightly edgy from his travel to being alert about the details of her business week. She knew he was calculating the opportunities they'd have to be alone before he returned to Wichita at the end of the week.

"No," she said finally, "but the newsletter going around features advertising from my vendors."

"The people you get your own supplies from?"

"Yes, like my bags of mulch, my seeds, and also the pottery that's sold in the shop," Daisy said.

Kenneth took his time to think about her response. In doing so, he was able to visualize what she'd be dealing with and how he might be able to help her achieve her goal of a successful event. In order to help, he needed to understand the various parts of her upcoming program. "Do you have categories of flowers or something like that?"

"Yes," Daisy said, pleased he was interested. He could easily have made life difficult by demanding more of her time than she could reasonably allow; people depended on her for guidance.

It was tough enough to squeeze a romantic interlude between her regular business and the side business of the garden show, but it would have been extremely tiresome to deal with a negative attitude from the man she loved.

For the most part, she and Kenneth were so compatible that she sometimes worried if what they shared was too good to be true under everyday conditions. This week would be a great proving ground. With fried nerves all around them, their generous natures would be tested, both in public and in private.

She said, "The competition for the roses is broken down into tea rose specimens, climbers, ramblers, floribundas, and minis. Each area has a class taught by one of my gardening club members. We'll all be very busy on the day of the event, but because of all the planning we did in advance, we feel prepared for whatever happens. Unless something freaky goes down, the garden show should be a success. Besides, from start to finish, the event should last for the morning only. We can all hang for that long."

Kenneth nodded his head. Daisy and her friends were taking the time to work out foreseeable trouble spots so that when the garden show was presented, the garden club members would be available for questions, answers, and education. Leave it to Daisy, he reasoned, to cram a lot into a very short time. She thought and worked in a concentrated format.

He expected that her one-day flower show would be unforgettable. How could it be anything else when its hostess was throwing her entire body and soul into the project? Kenneth figured he had a lot of catching up to do if he planned to help her keep the event fluent and trouble-free.

"So," he said, "those people who want to know more about climbers and ramblers can learn about them as opposed to learning about the tea roses?"

"Yes."

Daisy loved it when he came to visit, when he treated her as if she was the only person in the world who mattered. His presence filled every room with his own special brand of masculinity. In the truck, his confidence allowed her to let her own guard down. Soon they would be home, at her place.

There, in the bedroom, his shoes would rest enormous next to hers, his presence again reminding her of how good it felt to share her life, however briefly, with a man able to ease the ache of far too many nights spent alone. Soon they would have absolute privacy.

He blended his life to hers easily on the surface, when in truth he worked hard at getting along, at protecting a relationship he valued. In his line of work, Kenneth had learned to take nothing for granted, but it was the little, unconscious things that endeared him to her during his many brief, intense visits.

At the table in her kitchen, he ate twice as much as she did, which she found funny. In their downtime, he preferred to watch sporting events on television while she turned the set to the Home and Garden channel or to a channel that featured classic films. She relished their differences. It was hard to imagine life without him.

Over six feet tall and two hundred pounds, single and childless, Kenneth excelled in his career as a private investigator, a part of his life that he generally sheltered her from by not talking about it.

As far as Daisy was concerned, the only problem with his career was that his business was located in Wichita, Kansas, a profitable location for him. As much as she wanted him near, she had never asked him to make the sacrifice of relocating, one she knew she couldn't make herself. Guthrie was home and always would be.

Kenneth had been tempted to relocate to Guthrie in order to be closer to Daisy but had not given in to the impulse. He was not a rash person; there were definite signs that he should tread forward in their relationship on slow but steady feet. Daisy wanted her own space, and no matter how many times he asked her to marry him, she refused.

She refused because she believed that marriage was a lifetime commitment. She was afraid of making a mistake, something that would be easy to do in the company of such a charismatic man as Kenneth, a man who found part of his attraction in the fact that she was not immediately accessible to him on any given day. Distance, for him, added flavor to the pot.

She was one of those people that believed absence made the heart grow fonder, and while it was true that she cared deeply for Kenneth, it was also true that she believed marriage would diminish the ultimate authority she held over her own life: she would forevermore think in terms of two instead of one, his opinions and feelings as well as her own. Life would no longer be simple.

It was much easier to focus on her own wants and needs within the comfort of the home and business she'd built for herself. . . . It was the beautiful sense of companionship, of oneness, that she could never duplicate without Kenneth. It was that scrumptious singular way she felt when they were alone together, like now, that let her know he was more than too good to be true; he was a definite keeper.

Still, fear of failure was in the back of her mind, a reality check that kept her grounded. Beautiful things were sometimes broken. She was strong on her own, but once she fully opened herself and her life to include Kenneth, would she be as strong if he changed his mind about them, if he left her someday? It was a leap of faith she wasn't ready to commit to.

She enjoyed the electrifying shot of energy she received every time he stepped off the plane and into her waiting arms. The only other thing in her life with the ability to make her nerves jangle was coffee, something she drank at least a dozen times every day. She liked her coffee hot, black, and strong, qualities she also attributed to the only man in her life.

Kenneth made her feel treasured and desirable, whether she wore makeup or not, had on jeans or a sundress. He and coffee were her two favorite vices. She wondered how her lover would feel if he knew that she considered her growing devotion somewhat of a blemish on what had, until now, been an easygoing lifestyle. To be her own boss in every way was, for Daisy, a true turn-on. She excelled with power.

Her business was successful because she put her heart into the running of it. Kenneth diverted that energy from the business to himself. In the past, nothing and no one had been allowed to interfere with the running of her garden shop. The way caffeine kept her addicted to coffee, power kept her addicted to business, and now, love kept her addicted to Kenneth Gunn. To date, she hadn't been able to get enough.

Once they arrived at her house, they quickly settled into the kitchen, their usual way of transition between whatever he'd been dealing with before visiting and whatever she was putting aside to make room for him. It was a neutral zone.

At the kitchen counter, Daisy filled a paper filter with fresh-ground gourmet coffee. The day before, she had bought whole beans from D.G.'s Coffee, a two-story turn-of-the-century brick building in Guthrie, something she did every other week as a special treat for herself. Since she and Kenneth were going to sit on the porch for a while, Daisy put the coffee in commuter mugs. This way it would stay hot in a container that was easy to carry around.

Kenneth always liked to walk through Daisy's gardens to see her current projects, something he'd do first thing in the morning. Over the last six weeks, she'd been working on a cottage garden that was crammed with annuals and perennials.

His favorite thing to do when she planted a new

garden was to look for garden follies, little yard orna-ments she tucked away in the flower beds. Since his last visit, she had set toad houses on the ground, one beneath a perennial rudbeckia and one beneath a bi-ennial foxglove, something he'd noticed because of the bright security light outside near the place he'd parked the truck. His deep interest pleased her.

"I love June," Daisy said. It was clear from her tone and body language that she loved Kenneth in June, as well.

"Me too," he said as he gazed through the windows in her casually decorated white kitchen. Everything about Daisy's home and life was casual, and yet the way she put it all together made her home and her life as gratifying to Kenneth as old-fashioned comfort food: meat loaf and mashed potatoes, fried chicken and collard greens. "Your gardens are like pictures in a magazine. I've never seen anything like them."

"Thank you. By now, you know how much I like theme gardening. It's a great way to experiment with patterns and colors."

Kenneth smiled at her. "You've definitely done that."

After the modern feel of Wichita, Kenneth always enjoyed the stepping-back-in-time feeling he got whenever he returned to Guthrie, a city that focused more on renovation of existing properties than the construction of new ones, a habit that helped to make the city charming and unique.

He hoped the city would continue to grow tastefully and gracefully. He expected this because its neigh-boring city, Edmond, was creeping into traditionally rural areas. He and Daisy enjoyed Sunday drives through the new neighborhoods, homes that were edging toward the main city of Guthrie.

Daisy believed the town was changing for the better, slowly, but definitely changing. There were children who spent many years away from home only to return to Guthrie to settle and retire, bringing with them the knowledge and skill they had learned from other parts of the country and the world.

She believed that those returning were the town's anchors because they remembered the good times, the days when there was more than one public swimming pool, more than one movie theater, and many things for all ages to do, from shopping to living to recreation. It was Daisy who pointed out that Guthrie was becoming a mecca for artists with talents ranging from music to painting to sculpting and in her case, gardening.

She approached gardening as a form of recreation and as an art form, which was one of the reasons her gardening club was such a success and why her rose nursery and garden shop had become a tourist attraction: Daisy helped customers choose gardens to fit their home landscape designs. This work was a natural extension of her own home landscape designs.

When she did this, she considered climate, topography, and how the yard space would be used by a given family. For example, front yard gardens tended to be more formal and neighborhood friendly than backyard gardens, which tended to meld with the natural habits of the family that lived in the house. This proved a successful strategy, one that increased word-of-mouth business sales and repeat customers.

Kenneth believed that there were no two homes exactly alike in Guthrie, even though many shared the same type of window casements or basic design structure. This was definitely not a cookie-cutter-styled town.

Overall, what Kenneth saw in this part of central Oklahoma was opportunity. A man could make his mark and have it stand for generations. Daisy had done this with her business.

While it was true that many people planted vegetable gardens or planted crops, there were some Guthrians who planted flowers simply for pleasure and recreation. Daisy was one of those gardeners, and from what Kenneth had seen from his drives around town, her gardens were spectacular.

Her gardens were exceptional because they fit perfectly with her home, so that outside gardens became extensions of the rooms inside her house. Guests like Kenneth were made to feel as if they had found some sort of harmonic living zone that was free from personal problems and public politics.

At Daisy's place, more than beauty reigned supreme; there existed a profound state of tranquillity, as if being on her property was in some way a commune with nature so wonderful that it bordered on a personal meditation.

For him, this setting was a much-needed respite from his daily life. It was no wonder she chose not to move away from Guthrie. Daisy was one of those people who turned her house and property into a private oasis, a verdant place that satisfied nearly all her needs. Kenneth felt welcome.

The feeling started with Daisy's home itself. It was a two-thousand-square-foot country-styled farmhouse complete with a porch that ran the length of the front of the house. There was a detached double-size garage that had a red climbing rosebush sprawled along the east side. The house was painted yellow with white trim. White shutters bordered more than a dozen windows. The roof was tiled in blue. No other home in Guthrie came close to this one.

Daisy's home was the only classic farmhouse with this particular set of colors. Built in 1900, the floors and house were made of wood. The rectangular shape of the house ran north and south, the entrance door facing west. The setting was friendly and the front yard overflowed with flowers that bloomed from spring until fall. Seldom did her yard have nothing in bloom.

There were huge drifts of perennial and bulbs that were interspersed with annuals for variety and sharp contrasts of color. The overall mood of the house was neighborly and very relaxed. The driveway and walkways near the house were curved and made of either brick or stone. There was no cement visible anywhere on the grounds. Even the foundation of Daisy's house was made of old stone.

Huge trees afforded the house seclusion from the highway it faced and provided protection from the setting sun. There was a short picket fence on either side of the driveway and in front of the matching fences were lavender shrubs, a group of four-foot-tall foxglove, and white iceberg roses that smelled divine, even in the dark.

On the outer sides of the picket fences were weeping willow trees, their bottom fringes trimmed evenly above the ground so that when Daisy manicured the lawn on her riding John Deere mower, she didn't have to duck her head. The other benefit of trimming the willow trees was to make sure that sunlight reached the iceberg roses, which needed at least half a day of sun every day.

However, it was the gardens, not the color scheme, that set Daisy's home apart from every other home in Guthrie. She used theme gardens as a way to experiment with color and placement. Her songbird garden was composed of circular shapes that created an intimate setting from the house and other gardens.

There was a white bistro table with two chairs set beneath a mature dogwood tree that had lovely pink flowers when in bloom. On the table, in a decorative tin box, were two binoculars, a pair for Daisy and a pair for a friend if she had one visiting with her.

The binoculars were used to study the birds in the natural habitat she'd created for them. In the songbird garden, there were birdbaths, a rotting log for woodpeckers to play with, hummingbird feeders, nectar-rich plants, and plants that produced edible berries. It was a songbird's paradise.

For relaxation, Daisy and Kenneth often sat in the songbird garden to listen to the birds sing or to watch them play, a habit Kenneth had come to look forward to during his visits. There was a small grass garden that was made of ornamental grasses, which Kenneth would have called weeds until meeting Daisy.

She had an English garden, its focal point a classic-style gazebo. The large yard feature had a single entrance and was distinguished by its simple and traditional pattern, a configuration composed of eight sides and an overall area of roughly 160 square feet, just enough room to seat ten people comfortably.

Inside the gazebo was a white wrought-iron table set. All the furniture in Daisy's garden was white, the color she preferred to showcase her flowers and the subtle background of green grass. White was also phosphorescent in the twilight hours. For those reasons, Kenneth was able to enjoy her gardens by using only the light of the moon, which always seemed brighter there, in the country feel of Daisy's gardens.

In turn, Daisy watched Kenneth catalog the subtle changes to her home since his last visit. One thing she liked about him was his ability to be strong without being a know-it-all bully. He knew a lot, but he didn't force his opinions or his attitude down her throat. He listened and he allowed her to talk whenever she wanted to say what was on her mind.

When she looked at Kenneth, she clearly saw his twin personality traits of absolute courage and absolute self-control. This was power. As always with supremely self-reliant people, there was the negative side of power, the ability to ruin what was created in the first place. A man like Kenneth was his own best friend or his own worst enemy.

Coming from a sound family background and normal upbringing, Kenneth was secure and emotionally stable. He was rugged, naturally charming, and confident. She enjoyed his take-charge attitude and appreciated the way his sense of humor kept him from being overbearing.

His empire was his private detective agency and his Achilles' heel was his habit of performing pro bono work for people he considered underdogs, those who were weak or perhaps just temporarily down on their luck.

In this regard, Kenneth was like Daisy, whom many claimed had a bleeding heart. Daisy took in stray animals, mostly cats and dogs, fed them, and took them to the animal shelter if there was no matching description for the animal in the lost-and-found section of the *Guthrie News Leader,* her hometown newspaper.

"Found any new strays lately?" Kenneth asked. His tone was teasing.

She rolled her eyes. People sometimes delivered stray animals to her door when the shelter was closed. Kenneth had witnessed this once and had been asking her this question ever since. "No."

He leaned over and kissed her, just because he loved her. "I've always wondered how you manage to keep Cutie Pie from getting jealous of the time you spend with other animals." Cutie Pie was Daisy's four-year-old German shepherd, a big dog with black and nearly white fur. Daisy had rescued the animal from a pet adoption service on a whim. She and the shepherd fell in love at first sight.

Daisy shrugged. "Cutie Pie knows that when I put a stray in the holding pen, it isn't permanent and that I'm trying to help. She might feel differently if I took on another animal full-time, but for the most part, she's secure and happy. I spend a lot of time with her."

Kenneth had seen them in action together. The dog followed Daisy around the gardens to keep an eye on her. "It shows. She's very loyal."

"I'm lucky to have her."

Kenneth ran his eyes over Daisy's attire and thought, *I'm lucky to have* her. She wore a soft knit capri pantsuit in a light peach color. The fabric was lightweight and clung to her every curve. Her sandals were slim and gold. Her lipstick was a shimmery pink red, her other make-up very light and complementary to her skin. She looked like a bloom on the flowering confetti lantana she grew at the base of her mailbox.

She smelled as delightful as she looked, yet it was her eyes, sharp and inquisitive, that held his attention.

Her eyes were the windows into an intelligent mind. Right now, that energy was directed solely at him.

As much as he wanted to help her out of her pantsuit, he knew they had all night long to linger in each other's arms. One thing he never wanted to do was make her feel his main objective was to get her between the sheets. He wanted all of her, inside and out. They needed to finish off the parameters of this brief lovers' holiday. He said, "Tell me more about the garden show."

She chuckled softly over his ability to focus. This was not a man who rushed things, but rather a man who felt comfortable setting boundaries, who preferred not to mix business with pleasure. So did she.

She said, "I'm having it at the fairgrounds here in town. Kandi Kane will attend and present awards. She's the keynote speaker."

Kenneth refilled their commuter mugs with coffee and turned off the electric pot. Even though they were planning to spend their night making love, he'd have been too wired to sleep anyway. He never could understand how Daisy was able to drink coffee at 10:00 P.M. and be fast asleep in bed by 11:00 P.M. "What a name," he said. "Kandi."

"Yeah, and believe me, that woman is anything but sweet."

Kenneth heard the disgruntled note in her tone and was curious. "Why are you inviting her, then?"

Daisy's shrug was eloquent. "She's a celebrity garden buff. A good word from Kandi Kane is like manna from heaven. Sales quadruple when she gives a green light on a business. That's a boon for a retail shop like mine."

Kenneth wanted to understand Daisy's reservations

about the celebrity speaker. "Then what's the problem with her?"

"She's a terrible gossip. Nasty. She acts as if she's mad at the world or something, but she writes wonderful stories. I want one of those stories written about my business."

Kenneth was surprised this would be an issue for such a brief encounter. "What does she do when she's rude?"

"Kandi makes ugly comments about people's private lives and she dishes out personal details along with her garden column, which is regionally syndicated. When she wrote about the upcoming garden show in her column, she mentioned that I took in a stray man last year, a man I knew nothing about and kept all to myself until he was feeling better. She made it seem as if I was daft and more than a little bit desperate."

Kenneth knew Daisy was referring to the way they'd met. Two thugs had beaten him up and left him for dead in her garden. Unfortunately, his beating was severe enough to leave him unconscious, a condition that led to a brief bout of amnesia. Daisy had taken care of him until he'd recovered mentally and physically. His recovery had been complete.

Afterward, she had helped him solve the murder mystery he had been investigating before the beating. Since then, they had been engaged in a long-distance relationship. Kenneth was tired of the arrangement. He wanted more, needed more.

Even though she loved him, Daisy liked living on her own and wasn't in a hurry to change her lifestyle dramatically by getting married. This elusive quality about her kept Kenneth on his toes. He was obsessed with her in a way he'd never been with another woman. She wasn't playing hard to get—she really was.

Kenneth said, "Tell me more about Kandi Kane." He wanted to be armed in case the woman proved dangerous.

"Kandi is gorgeous. Dark-skinned, flawless complexion, supershort black hair that she curls tight to her head. She wears trademark boots she orders from Sorrell Custom Boots right here in town."

This startled him. "Kandi is from Guthrie?"

"No," Daisy explained. "She's from some little town in the middle of nowhere, but she met someone with a pair of Sorrell boots on and loved them so much she wanted a pair just like them."

Kenneth had never seen Daisy wear anything on her feet other than gardening shoes, tennis shoes, or the occasional sandals. "Do you have any of these boots?"

"I commissioned the artist to make me a pair of kangaroo boots in a design we worked out together. She's got a waiting list of customers but she expects to have my boots ready in time for Christmas. It's my present to myself."

"What's the design on your boots?"

"There's a cluster of daisies tied with a ribbon and on the ribbon are the words *Daisy's Rose Nursery and Garden Shop.*"

Kenneth shook his head and smiled while doing it. "Guthrie is full of newsworthy people. I don't think I've met a dull friend of yours yet."

"That's another reason why I like D.G.'s Coffee. No one is ever a stranger there and it's an unofficial haunt of artists."

Kenneth was silent a few seconds. "Is that where you bought the new birdhouse?"

Daisy's eyes lit up. "You noticed!"

"Of course. It's why I like to walk through your gardens whenever I come to visit. It lets me know what you've been up to and I like seeing the seasonal changes in your yard. The birdhouse is a nice addition to your porch ornaments."

"I think so, too. I had the artist coat the overall piece in a weather-resistant veneer since the front of my house gets so much sun."

The birdhouse was an octagon shape that the artist had crackled and painted an antique white. It had a purple and green vine painted on it and rested on an antique white pedestal that Daisy had nailed onto the porch to keep it from being knocked over by the wind.

On either side of the birdhouse were a pair of stark-white rocking chairs made of wood. The cushions on the chairs had the same purple and green vines the artist had painted on the birdhouse. Items such as these made Daisy's place unique.

Kenneth said, "It all fits. Your hobbies and friends and favorite haunts are all connected into a circle."

Daisy hadn't thought about it before but Kenneth was right.

An artist himself, he had built a bench for Daisy that wrapped around the scarlet maple tree in her backyard.

"But it's more than that," he said. "You have a great eye for putting a variety of things together, mismatched things. You don't just throw plants haphazard in the yard, you have a pattern and shape to what you do."

She smiled. "So do you. Speaking of pattern and shape, why don't you go ahead and turn part of the garage into a workshop for yourself? You could make birdhouses to sell in the garden shop. They'd be a big hit. I'd sell them with packets of flower seeds known for attracting local birds. I can hear the cash register ringing now."

Kenneth laughed. "Just about everything you do gets somehow connected to your garden. The people you meet. The places you go. Everything. Maybe that's part of your success. You love what you do and you do what you love."

"Don't make me sound so cherry-pie sweet and so . . . organized. Basically, I just go with the flow. I can't stand Kandi Kane but I'm excited about what she can do for my business. If you could build birdhouses, I'd be able to premiere them after Kandi's big write-up in the papers. I'm already selling wind chimes and outside wall thermometers.

"There are people who want me to sell trees, but they take up too much space. I refer them to my friend Robin Brandon out on Highway 33. She refers people to me and so we help each other in business that way. Kind of like how D.G.'s Coffee and French Underground help each other."

Kenneth laughed at her. "You and your coffee. I'd hate to see what would happen to you if you tried to stop drinking it. Have you ever tried?"

"Once. I had a colossal headache when I did and I've never tried since. I used to drink Folgers coffee but then I sampled some gourmet coffee and got hooked. The more I drink, the more I want. That's how I think of you, too. The more time I spend with you, the more time I want to spend."

"Marry me."

"No."

"Don't you want children?"

"No."

"Don't you want me to be with you every day and night?"

"No."

"You're a tough cookie, Daisy."

She wished they didn't have to go this route, but like the business of the garden show, they had to discuss this, too. This was a conversation about their future. If they couldn't make a case for one, this might wind up being their last time together. Neither of them could afford to pour feelings into a bottomless pit.

"I'm happy," she said. "I don't believe a woman has to be married with children in order to feel good. I have a career and a marvelous lifestyle."

"So if it ain't broke, don't fix it." He wasn't being nice.

"Right."

He stared her down, as if he dared her to deny the truth. "I know you get lonely some nights. One day we'll be old, Daisy."

"I'll be ready when the time comes and I'll feel good knowing I lived life on my own terms and that in the process I made other people happy along the way. Live and let live, that's my motto."

He frowned at her. "I could walk out of your life right now and you wouldn't protest, would you?"

She folded her arms across her chest. "Of course I'd protest, but I don't want you here unless you want to be here. The harmony you feel when you come to my place is because I don't fight the flow of things in life. What is, is. Like a friend of mine says, heaven and hell happen every day of our lives. We can choose to be happy or miserable. I tackle one day at a time and in that one day, I do my best to be happy. When I'm happy, it makes other people happy."

Her honesty hurt but it was real. "You keep life uncomplicated. I suppose that's the other thing about you that I find attractive after the hustle of Wichita. It's that black or white style of thinking of yours that intrigues me. You don't deal in gray areas."

She forced her breathing to even out. Communication was one thing, fighting was something else. She didn't like to fight. "Gray areas are for people who straddle the fence. I'm not one of those people."

"Is that why you don't practice an active religious life?"

"God created the day and every day is good, even though on occasion bad things will happen in the course of any given day. I don't sweat over things I can't control, which is everything outside my body and mind. I don't want to own you and I don't want to be owned by you. That's why I won't marry you, Kenneth."

The idea was like a chip on her shoulder, a big one. "Daisy," he said, "marriage isn't ownership."

"It is."

"Break this down for me because I totally disagree."

She expelled her breath in a huff. "You automatically get half of everything that is mine and the same goes for me with whatever you have. Marriage means we own the right to see each other naked, happy, sad, or whatever before anybody else does. It means you'd own part of my time and part of my space. I like my time. I like my space."

"You're talking about freedom," he said, seeking clarification.

"Yes. I like my freedom. I like being in a relationship with the front door open."

He rocked back in his seat. "Chicken."

She unfolded her arms and placed her elbows on the table. "Maybe. But why is it okay for a guy to be single forever and not a woman? Why is it okay for a man to choose a career over children and not be considered selfish or a freak of nature the way some women are?"

"I don't know, Daisy. I just know that being married means I alone would have the right to call you mine—and no other man. I want that right."

"See? You'd own me."

He thought she was being ridiculous about this ownership business and it showed on his face. "Maybe we should talk about this later."

"I won't be changing my mind."

"Anything is possible."

"I suppose if I can get Kandi Kane down here to little old Guthrie, then you're probably right."

His grin was lopsided, half serious, half not. "You've got a real knack for turning lemons into lemonade."

She batted her lashes like film diva Mae West. "You mean this weird conversation we're having?"

She really was being ridiculous. "We're having a fight. A controlled fight, but a fight all the same. I want to get married and you don't."

"It ain't broke," Daisy said, referring to their nearly year old relationship.

Kenneth took her by the hand and pulled her outside to the bistro set in the songbird garden. He needed fresh air before he said something he might regret. A lighted path led their way. It smelled lovely in the dark, like roses and lemons and peppermint, things he couldn't see or touch without the sun to guide him. They held hands. "Tell me about this garden show and what I can do to help."

She was relieved to change the subject. "We'll need platforms and tables set up. Mostly, I'll need help with crowd control after the initial muscle part is over with."

"Muscle part as in lifting and hauling?"

"Yes. I'd also like a few plywood tables made with two-by-four legs that I'll cover with white plastic. Exhibitors will be able to showcase their specimens on them."

"So you need a carpenter, too."

"Exactly."

Kenneth liked to wear black the way fictional private investigator Kinsey Millone wore jeans, sneakers, or boots with a tank top or turtleneck as all-purpose gear. Black kept his travel bag at a minimum and his clothing always interchangeable. If he went to a restaurant after a day of work and had on a black top with black jeans, he could switch the jeans to black slacks and come out all right. Black would be a problem if he was working with wood and sawdust.

To save packing time and hassle, he kept a set of clothes at Daisy's place, so he knew he'd be able to find something more suitable for carpentry work. The issue of what the garden show would involve and how he could help now resolved, Kenneth was ready to end the evening in Daisy's arms. Their walk through the garden was the perfect segue.

The songbird garden was in full serenade and he marveled at the sounds. He admired the woman who'd created such a space with her own hands and imagination. Kenneth suppressed a sigh of frustration. He was in love with a woman who refused to marry him, a woman who didn't want children, a woman who didn't need a man to validate her self-worth, a woman he couldn't get out of his mind.

The chaste kiss she'd placed on his lips after he walked off the airplane was like the first lick of his favorite ice cream. One lick was not enough. He used his tone of voice to tell her he wanted to lick her from head to toe. "I was exhausted before I got here. I drank coffee on the plane to jazz myself up, but seeing you for the first time in six weeks is like mainlining six shots of espresso."

Daisy laughed. "Espresso makes my hair stand on end."

Kenneth laughed, too. "You drink so much coffee as a rule that it amazes me you can't drink espresso."

"Me too. But every time I try it, my skin crawls with the willies and the hairs on my arms stand up."

He said again, just as he pulled her close within the circle of his arms, "We're gonna be up all night."

While Daisy and Kenneth did the wild thing between hot and sweaty sheets, Kandi Kane was psyching herself up to be the main attraction at Daisy's grand garden show special event. She, too, stood over a garden—a courtyard full of weeds. In the morning, she'd drive to Guthrie. In the morning, she'd have a pot to stir, people to rile, nerves to shatter. She only wished she had a more earthshaking name to go with her current hard-core attitude.

Kandi hated her name but she loved her mother so she never changed it. Instead, she did everything she could to deny the manufactured sweetness her name implied. She was tough, smart, considered a bitch by many of her peers, but what she lacked in the way of true friends she made up for in the way of accolades from prominent leaders in the professional garden community.

She knew her fauna from her flora, and her specialty was in the selection of rather obscure garden shows in the seldom-heard-of small towns that dominated the Southwest and lower southeastern states. She agreed to do the Guthrie event for garden show novice Daisy Rogers as a favor to the friend of a friend of her daughter, Sugar Kane.

Sugar had attended Langston University in Langston, Oklahoma, where she'd earned a degree in business administration. While at Langston, Sugar had met and befriended one of Daisy's former employees, a handyman named Chester Whitcomb, a man whom Kandi had been shocked to learn was arrested and recently convicted of murdering an undercover policewoman, a friend of Kenneth's.

It wasn't until after Kandi accepted the assignment to cover the Guthrie garden show that she and Sugar made the connection of Daisy with Chester Whitcomb. It was a small world and a place where Kandi had learned quickly in life that a woman could run from her destiny but she could not hide, a fact she was chagrined to discover when she named her only child a name as silly as her own: Sugar.

Quirky names ran in the maternal side of Kandi's family. Her own mother, whose maiden name was Flowers, was named Sunnie. Sunnie grew fields of sunflowers in various heights and colors, which she harvested and sold to flower markets and craft stores throughout the middle and eastern states.

Kandi had left the family home, gotten pregnant by

a man named William Kane, IV, who ran off with his father's secretary, a former stripper named Bootsie who made sure Kandi knew of the affair by sending her a nasty video of herself and William having sex on his father's mahogany office desk. This was while Kandi was pregnant.

Kandi knew the baby she carried was a girl because she willed it to be a girl and she crooned all the time to her unborn daughter, saying things like, "It's gonna be all right, sugar. I love you, sugar."

When her daughter was born in the company of Sunnie Flowers and the cabdriver they'd hired to take them to the hospital, a driver named Sugar, Kandi knew it was destiny, the reason she named her daughter Sugar.

She figured that as long as her daughter didn't marry a man with the surname Pie or Plum, she would be all right. As far as Kandi was concerned, destiny was at it again, which gave her more than fifteen minutes of serious thought, the reason she was staring at a weed-infested garden in the middle of the night. Of one thing Kandi Kane was certain: there were no accidents in life.

TWO

Sunday afternoon

Daisy and Kenneth were sharing a swing beneath the shade of a redbud tree. Holding hands, listening to the sounds of nature, they were heavy into their own thoughts. As much as she liked to have a good time with Kenneth when he came to visit her in Guthrie, Daisy also liked to stay on track with her business. She accomplished this by focusing on her goals, those private scoring points that stemmed largely from doing whatever it took to keep her garden shop in the black. Kenneth was a serious sidetrack because whenever he came around, she just wanted to play, day and night.

In order to stay on top of business, she steered away from the distractions posed by the needs of other people. She was constantly invited to attend this function or that function, to speak at this group or that group, constantly asked to serve on tourist recruiting committees and fund-raisers. A popular woman in town, both in social and professional circles, she was often in demand.

If she'd joined every conversation or function to which she'd been invited, she'd weaken the energy re-

quired to stay on top of her game—the crafting of
fine, custom gardens, the nurturing of sturdy, healthy
plants, the education of a buying public who found
her business a comfort and pleasure, which was, in
turn, the external view of her own happiness. Kenneth made her feel good on the inside. Eyes closed,
head resting against his shoulder, she squeezed his
hand. He squeezed her right back, even though he,
too, was lost in thought.

There was so much to think about.

Staying on track kept Daisy's days from running together and her seasons in order, kept her in touch
with her personal values, her intuition, herself. For
Daisy, this approach to living and working, this intense concentration on personal solitude and
professional longevity was a meditation, a way of ex-
periencing time in motion. Rarely was she frustrated
against time because it moved too fast or too slow. For
Daisy, time was time, infinite, real as air, soothing as
water, never circular or linear. It just . . . was.

In this detached way of thinking, Daisy was able to
satisfy her basic needs; seldom did she feel cornered
and trapped by her work, which was why she chose
not to wear a watch; clock-watching tended to rein-
force boredom, to dissect the day into its tiniest bits
and pieces, forcing her to think about the precise
movement of time rather than its overall flow.

Precise movement included the tedious watching of
seconds or hours, but the overall flow had to do with
the general way she felt by the end of the workday, either pleasantly pleased by the repetitious work,
terribly bored, or overwhelmed by exhaustion.

In this way, Daisy experienced time as a process versus an irritation. She wasn't rushing to get somewhere

or meet someone or fill her life with people and things she didn't need. This attitude made it possible for her to start things from scratch, to build a sound future from the ground up, to live well, and to live strong.

Thinking quietly and thoroughly, living thoughtfully, in harmony with her environment, enabled her to make solid choices, which in turn made her a valuable and wise friend, to herself and to those people she deemed necessary to quality living: her mother, Rita, Zenith Braxton, Cinnamon Hartfeld, Mr. Dillingsworth, her garden club, and . . . Kenneth.

He alone interfered with the solitude Daisy so carefully constructed and carefully protected. He shifted her thoughts outward, away from herself as an individual to herself as part of a couple. As a couple, there were issues of possession to resolve, such as personal freedom, personal boundaries, personal power, personal air space, all that business about being one, when Daisy already felt one in herself.

She didn't feel like half a person and therefore she didn't need a man to make her feel whole. Like time, Kenneth was just . . . Kenneth. He was easygoing, protective, kind, attentive, hers for the asking, hers for the taking.

In his own right, he was a force to be reckoned with, not a man to be controlled or manipulated or made to bow down in a show of submission. His power was his and her power hers, as long as they both were careful. It was tough for Daisy to be careful when Kenneth so easily broke her concentration, as he did now, stroking her palm softly with the rough underside of his huge thumb.

Being so close beside him, having him around from dawn to dawn, made her think of sex and satisfaction, of laughter and fun times, a playmate instead of a helpmate. His friendship was an asset, something she wanted to keep and to cherish, which is why she made space for him in her life whenever he had time to spare.

Being with Kenneth stopped time for Daisy. She lost track of minutes and hours and days, which made her wary when she considered the future. She couldn't afford to become a clock-watcher, because watching the clock would make her feel ordinary, when normally she felt very enlightened, empowered, and fully alive, as tied to her work and her home as the name on the sign above her business, DAISY'S ROSE NURSERY AND GARDEN SHOP. It was her world, her strength, and until meeting Kenneth Gunn, her everything.

In her line of business, it was easy to get caught up in the miniplanet she'd created, the place where her work and her living zones operated side by side, the only separation between them the one she devised in her mind and enforced with her own free will. Nothing was complicated until Kenneth came along—not one thing.

Maintaining a simple, graceful lifestyle during the hustle of everyday life took subjective reasoning, supported by decisive, goal-oriented acts. This willpower allowed her to be independent and self-contained, a woman who wasn't needy, a woman able to give the best parts of herself without submerging her desires or her identity for the sake of someone else's happiness. For Daisy, this spelled success.

It took determination as well as risk to be a successful entrepreneur. Daisy wasn't one of those people who started businesses and sold them once the thrill of start-up was over. For her, Daisy's Rose Nursery and Garden Shop was her life's work, the thing she did to keep on living and thriving in a world where, for many, time moved too fast and good things were too easily replaced with better items the first minute better diversions came along.

Her life was more like an old-time garden, one that adapted to the ravages of weather, sometimes dying to the ground as a tree and reemerging as a shrub, or even a rose that began as a tea hybrid one year only to revert to its native state as a climber the next. A veteran or master gardener was gifted at adapting, at designing ways to help a garden flourish despite the adversity of insects, sun, wind, frost, and foraging animals.

In Daisy's world, she was the master, the expert veteran, and she relished her ability to pick and choose from the best life had to offer. Right now, the best thing life had to offer her was Kenneth Gunn. The balancing act between being alone and being part of a couple was bittersweet.

In the garden, there was time to meditate on the real world, to gain insight into the meaning of dreams, a place to forge fresh ideas, to redefine and maintain self-control, to provide comfort to herself and ultimately to others, as she had done when she found and met Kenneth. It was hard to imagine almost a year had gone by since they'd first met.

Since then, her garden and their relationship had grown more beautiful, more strongly rooted. Roots served as anchors to the earth; they harnessed water, stored food, were essential to health and vitality, to prosperity. For these reasons, Daisy herself was rooted.

Her garden and her home were similar anchors and now, in Kenneth, she'd found fruit. He was firm of flesh, dark of skin, unblemished, and reminiscent of a Fuji apple—not too sweet, not too sour, just right. He wasn't ordinary, but neither was he exotic. He was just right—not too needy, not too dominating, but very much himself, in control, self-contained, loving, and lovable, as committed to his lifestyle as she was to hers.

The trouble for Daisy wasn't in wanting Kenneth, but wanting to share her already full and balanced life with someone else. Once she let him in, she would meld and merge with him, give some of herself and some of her happiness over to him. And then where would her business be? Certainly, it would suffer, because her attentions would be diverted, a little for herself, a little for Kenneth, and the rest for the garden shop.

Number one, her business, even though it was her hobby, was also her source of food on her table at home. Number two, regardless of how long she worked or how difficult the occasional customer turned out to be, her garden shop was generally an uplifting experience for her and the people she shared it with on a regular basis.

Her customers had become her companions, just as royal purple salvia was a nice complement to the perfect peach roses in her garden. Her customers had become her means for communication, her method of not truly being alone even if she was, on occasion, lonely in ways that a woman without a steady partner can be.

Most of her customers existed in the gray space of her life, the place where they were more than casual acquaintances but less than true friends. True friends dealt with the good and the bad, the laughing and the crying: the truth. Kenneth was this kind of friend, and Daisy was smart enough to realize that she didn't need to be married to him in order to hold on to that bond. All she had to do was be fair.

What Daisy worried about was territory. She liked her territory just the way it was, occasional loneliness and all. And the territory she liked best was simply herself. She wasn't one of those women who gave so much of themselves away that they had little left to feed their own souls. In herself, she felt complete, even without a husband, even without children. She had her business to thank for that peace of mind, her home, her dearest friends.

She rebelled when people said, "Just close up and leave early," when they wanted her to tag along to some social event that was spur-of-the-moment, and even though she would consider it, she rarely gave such proposals more than a cursory thought. Repeat business depended on her reliability.

She had set hours to keep, and by keeping those hours, she showed her clientele she was not a flighty person. When out-of-towners arrived to peruse her wares, they were disappointed to find upon arrival that she was closed. This is why she scheduled vacation during off-season months and kept consistant open hours.

Besides, without money she couldn't maintain her independence or feed the occasional stray animals she rescued, or satisfy her other, more playful appetites. She enjoyed water rafting each spring and fall, attending indoor rodeo functions at the Lazy E, or simply puttering around the house she'd lovingly restored. Because her life tended to be orderly and predictable, she liked to invent challenges, the flower show being such an invention.

This flower exhibition fed Daisy's desire to show Guthrie residents that flower growing was every bit as satisfying and rewarding and beneficial to the community as growing vegetables was to local wholesalers.

In a town where vegetable gardens and farm crops outnumbered landscapes heavily populated with flowers, this was no small task. A successful event would lead to greater publicity for her rose nursery and garden shop as well as more public education regarding the healing qualities of flower gardening.

There were many people who didn't realize that pansies could be candied in sugar and used to decorate cakes, or that jam could be made from roses, that lavender kept bugs away from linens, or that chamomile eased tired muscles and put an end to headaches.

Education, she had discovered, was the way to encourage strictly vegetable gardeners to experiment with flowers, beginning by adding a few easy things to plant among their vegetable favorites, such as allowing clematis vines to stretch to the top of an obelisk set among the leafy green vegetable section of the garden.

The possibilities of beauty for the table and for the home, whether indoors or out, were absorbing to Daisy. This fascination is what captured and held those people who were skeptical, the elderly in particular. She liked winning new customers in the same way a gambler liked winning at slot machines—eventually, constant effort paid off.

There were many elders in her community who asked when she planned to stop playing around with her life and get down to some real business, such as graduating from college, raising a family, or getting a corporate job. Daisy brushed those comments aside with as much grace as she could muster. She wasn't playing around. She was for real.

She lived on twenty acres, which she owned outright. Her home and her business were paid for. She used cash for what she wanted and worked ten full months of each calendar year. She'd been to the Bahamas, had toured Europe, and had attended college just long enough to decide she wasn't cut out for the traditional road to success, which was entirely okay with her closest relatives.

Her mother had raised her to believe that she was born successful and that everything else in life was gravy. Daisy subscribed to this philosophy wholeheartedly and this style of thinking was the source of her professional satisfaction. As far as she was concerned, there was always more than one way to skin a cat, but the best way was to be true to her own God-given strengths and natural inclinations.

For starters, Daisy was a nonconformist. By dropping out of college, she had freed herself of the need to adapt to conventional standards. Bringing this subject up was as volatile among her elders as the discussion of religion or politics, other topics she avoided whenever possible. For Daisy, the concept of "live and let live" was a personal anthem.

She performed both random and specific acts of kindness throughout her day, every day. She donated money and time to her community; she was civic-minded when it came to good causes, such as rescuing stray animals off the street and Kenneth Gunn from her garden; she attended her own affairs and stayed true to the positive way she was raised.

With steadfast determination, she steered clear of the issues she couldn't change and preferred to experience people as they were instead of the way she wanted them to be, which was why she enjoyed Kenneth so much: He functioned in the same way.

In business, she'd quickly discovered that sports and gardening and weather were neutral zones. She kept up with the growth and progress of Guthrie High School athletes and attended home games during football and basketball seasons.

She hung the blue-and-white Guthrie Blue Jay mascot in the window of her shop as a way to express her community pride. In this manner, she was able to converse with husbands who waited for wives in the garden shop, or vice versa.

Instead of renovating old barns and other outbuildings to store equipment on her twenty-acre site, she invested in sturdy structures she had custom-built to suit her needs, so when local residents gave her a hard time about squandering her days in the yard or whatever, she smiled quietly and then deftly diverted conversation elsewhere. She knew what she was doing, even if busybodies around her did not.

The only formal education Daisy had regarding horticultural training was the apprenticeship she earned at her mother's side. A seasoned gardener in her own right, Rita Rogers specialized in medicinal herbs as well as floribunda roses, the classic white iceberg roses being her favorites.

In turn, Daisy's mother had learned from her own mother, and together the three women traced their flower gardening heritage all the way to rural Alabama, where Daisy's great-great-grandmother Hattie made her living as a laundress by day and a root doctor by night.

As a root doctor, Hattie devised tonics from assorted flowers and herbs she managed to grow year-round and was a godsend to poor southern families with little or no money for traditional medicine or professional doctors, especially during the Depression when so many families struggled to provide food and shelter for themselves.

As a result of her heritage, Daisy grew up with a deep understanding of nature, of the value of flowers for healing the body and for soothing the mind through their careful and systematic cultivation.

In the current generation, she excelled in plant growing as a source of beauty, and her specialty was not simply in growing roses for the garden or table, but helping home owners build gardens that suited individual taste and lifestyle, a popular service for new home buyers in the fast-growing Edmond community.

During the winter months, she designed home gardens on her computer for potential clients. However, it was her own private gardens that launched her secondary and quickly growing career, that of a landscape developer for small garden sites.

Daisy approached landscape development the same way an interior designer set out to enhance and decorate a customer's home, which was room by room. A room in a garden was generally a section devoted to a particular theme, a hummingbird garden for example, a butterfly garden, or an evening garden composed primarily of white flowers and plants with silver foliage.

When Daisy was finished with someone's garden, her deft ministrations with color and scale often made a small yard seem larger or a large yard more cozy than it did before she'd started the project. Unfortunately, her business was growing faster than she could handle on her own. The subsequent loss of total control was frightening. She needed help and she needed it bad.

What she wanted now was a reliable builder to construct and install garden features such as gazebos, playhouses, and pergolas. Her chosen source had to be reliable, had to care about quality, had to believe in her work as much as she did, someone like . . . Kenneth.

She broke her reverie to eye him with open avarice and said, "I want you to go into partnership with me."

His face was a perfect blank, though his eyes gleamed with interest. "I take it from the calculating stare in your eyes that you're thinking along the lines of business," he said.

His tone was cautious. As far as Kenneth was concerned, Daisy was fanatical about her gardening habits. Her single-minded attention to detail and micromanagement left her competition in the dust, and while it was true that he greatly admired her, Kenneth had no desire to be her whipping boy. He'd much prefer a marriage partnership; that way they could keep the careers they'd been enjoying all along.

She registered his caution but stuck to her objective. Daisy liked to win. After careful selection of the battles she fought, she rarely lost a fight. She cracked her knuckles and squared her shoulders. Although she spoke calmly, her grin was unholy. "I am."

She was so much shorter and smaller than he was, Kenneth felt like laughing at her cocky demeanor. Instead, he humored her by asking, "Is this related to the garden show?"

"Kind of. I started thinking about it after you volunteered to build and set up the props I'll need for the program," Daisy said. She didn't mind him coming at her sideways. Just as long as he entered the discussion without turning her down flat.

Kenneth took a deep breath and let it out slowly. He was on the verge of squashing his true feelings, but that wasn't his style. Truth was everything and everything had its own place in time, including this fight. Delaying the conversation wouldn't make the subject go away. Although it wasn't his custom to do so, Kenneth sighed long and hard.

"Look, Daisy," he said, then skimmed a hand over the back of his head with a palm big enough to hold a basketball. "I don't want to spoil our fun by going into business. In my experience, partnerships between friends who stay friends are rare. I want to stay friends. While it's true that I find your work interesting, I don't see myself managing plants for a living."

Her dark brown eyes narrowed into contemplative slits. He'd been brief and to the point. She countered in the same vein. "Translation. You don't want to feel as if you're working for me."

"Damn straight."

She knew full well he had a weakness for pro bono work. Anybody who did that was a sucker for a good cause, and no matter how she sliced it, her cause was definitely good. She tried a different tactic. "That's not what I'm proposing."

It was his turn to narrow his eyes. He knew she wasn't about to give up. Even though she sometimes appeared absentminded, evidenced by the way she lost track of time in the garden, he knew that when she focused, like now, she was sharp and decisive. Formidable.

He said, "What exactly are you proposing, then?" This time, his tone was more curious than cautious.

"I want you to build garden features and let me buy them from you wholesale," Daisy said, fast, as if she thought he might interrupt before she got all the words out. She should have known better. Anybody able to sit on surveillance for hours at a time had enough patience to listen to his girlfriend try to win him over in a fight she had no intention of losing.

She had him hooked. He asked, "What exactly are you talking about?"

Daisy explained, "I want you to build small bridges to use in water gardens, small playhouses that are made to look like miniature cottages, small potting sheds and potting tables with benches."

Kenneth's expression was an odd mix of interest and skepticism. "You really think there's a market for that sort of thing?"

"I do," she said. "Many of my customers ask me for those types of follies for their gardens. Recently, a woman asked if I could connect her with someone who knows how to build a miniature gazebo to go with her daughter's playhouse."

"I wouldn't be interested in owning a full-scale business," Kenneth said. A night owl by nature, he could conduct such a business after hours, sort of like a hobby. What she proposed could be done.

"I understand," she said. "It would mean cutting down on your P.I. work."

"Not necessarily," he admitted. "Just say I do go along with this idea of yours and I do start a business in Guthrie. It would take a lot of capital to get going."

He knew what he was talking about; he was an excellent carpenter. One reason for this was that he paid attention to the details of craftsmanship. A major detail was the use of quality building materials. At best, such supplies were costly. He couldn't afford to waste money.

She was getting excited and didn't care if it showed. "Okay. Good point. What if you worked on commission only? That way, you'd have start-up money for each project up front, like the retainer you get from a client to cover expenses once you start an investigation."

She had him there. "You've given this a lot of thought," he said.

"I have."

He sought some clarification on a subject that was near and dear to his heart. Other than sex with Daisy, it was the second major topic on his mind. "You still don't want to share a home together." He made this a statement, not a question.

"No."

He applied reason to their argument. "For an easy-going woman, Daisy, you're pretty stubborn on that issue. It would be simpler to live in the same house."

"Simple isn't always better," she countered. "I like having my own space, Kenneth. I like living alone. Besides, regardless of what you say, I know you like living alone, too."

He rubbed his chin with rough fingers, then lifted a brow in subtle agreement. "Living alone has its good points."

Daisy had spent a lot of time considering the pros and cons of maintaining a long-distance relationship with Kenneth. "For the price of your condo, you could buy a small house in Guthrie. I have plenty of land space and an outbuilding in the far back I use only for storage. We can clear it out for you to use as a studio. That way, you don't have to transport whatever you build and you can build whatever you want.

"Your work will always be on display and the gardeners who visit my shop will be able to see what you do. For you, it'll be free advertising. For me, it's a painless way to expand on my business. In your downtime, you can build things that are ready to go and sell. I've got a number of people interested in Adirondack furniture. I'm one of those people."

Kenneth's brain was ticking away at full speed as he considered the options Daisy presented so matter-of-factly. She was definitely a force to be reckoned with, all 120 pounds of her.

He could relocate to Guthrie and make a living doing the woodwork hobby he loved. As far as he knew, he would be the only person doing that type of work in town on a regular basis—a tempting thought.

Potentially, commissioned work could be done for anyone in the state of Oklahoma. Daisy's business would do the selling, he would do the building, and the customer would do the hauling off. "You make it all sound so easy," he said.

She tried to still her delight, lest he thought she was gloating, which of course she was. "It is."

Kenneth said, "Just stop what I'm doing in Kansas, relocate to Guthrie, and start a new business doing something as risky as making big dollhouses for little girls to play in with their friends?"

"That's exactly what I'm saying. You keep telling me that you want us to be together all the time. We can. You'll be able to do your thing and I'll be able to do mine. Our businesses would complement each other and not contradict. We'd each have our own space. I like that idea. Also, we'd be on hand to help each other out if we need to."

Kenneth laughed. "You mean, you'll hammer and glue right along with me? Kind of like a hired hand?"

"Sure. Just like you'd be around to help me with the heavy work in my garden when I need it. Variety is definitely the spice of life."

Realistic by nature, Kenneth maintained a practical approach to the discussion. "It's still risky, and working with the public as an artist is a very uncertain business."

"Working as a private detective is risky. It's how we met in the first place," Daisy said, remembering how Kenneth's enemies had beaten him up and left him for dead in one of the compost piles in her garden.

She had rescued him, helped him solve a vicious murder case, and eventually fallen in love with him. They had been together ever since. It was June and time for Daisy to review her plans for the way she would spend her winter season.

Each winter, she renovated her business in some way, starting with a deep cleaning, progressing to re-inforcement of the shelving, touching up whatever paint had been scuffed or scratched, and ultimately in upgrading her shelving, storage, and other methods of display.

The previous winter, she'd hired a local painter to create a mural of a rustic one-story cottage on the north wall of the garden shop, Thomas Kincade–style, surrounded by gardens so realistic, many of Daisy's customers said the flowers looked real.

In this painted garden, there were vines of purple clematis growing among the red roses. Very old and established wisteria framed the entrance to the cottage and a nearly impenetrable hedge of perfect iceberg roses nestled against the base of the house on four sides. Among the star jasmine that fell over the split-rail fence in front of the vintage white cottage was the artist's name, which was written in script so lavish in design, it was almost unreadable.

The same artist, a sixteen-year-old high school student named Regina, had designed Daisy's business cards. Daisy had commissioned Regina to paint a weeping willow tree with a pair of little black girls in ribbons and ponytails swinging on a board seat attached to the tree with honey-colored rope.

The girls in the swing represented herself and her sister, Miranda. At age six, one year older than Daisy, Miranda had been hit and killed when she ran into the street to save a stranger's dog. A witness to the horrible accident, Daisy hadn't been able to help her sister, but she'd been able to save many dogs and other stray animals ever since.

Many people, including her mother, had expected Daisy to become a veterinarian. She hadn't. Saving strays was something she felt compelled to do, a sort of homage to her sister. However, it was her mother's garden and love that had saved Daisy. In her mother's garden, Daisy had been restored and made to feel whole.

Perhaps because it was the garden that fed her mother's own bruised spirit after the death of her eldest child, a death that had been the catalyst for the separation and eventual divorce between herself and Daisy's father, Templeton Rogers.

During her parents' separation and divorce, Daisy had built her first garden, without any help or guidance from her mother, who was distracted at the time. That first garden had led to another, which in turn had led Daisy to meet Regina over the fence that separated their houses.

Regina, who had moved with her family from Coyle, Oklahoma, to Guthrie, had been sitting on a tree stump in her own backyard, sketch pad in hand, as she recorded Daisy's first garden, ripe now with age and full of scent and color, on paper.

Thinking of the mural now gave Daisy an idea for the winter season, even though that time of year was several months away. She would dangle wind chimes on the painted porch and place handcrafted butterflies among the foxglove that grew along the faux painted steps of the cottage.

That way, when customers admired the design and wanted to take something home with them as a reminder of their visit, she would be able to discreetly suggest wind chimes and butterflies, simply by displaying them so creatively. Daisy discovered that she sold more of her knickknacks when she showed customers how they could be used in their own homes and gardens.

Because of this sales strategy, she was convinced any work Kenneth designed in the way of garden ornaments would sell quite well, especially if the prices were fair and easy to manage by ordinary people, customers she wanted to come back to the garden shop again.

Now that Kenneth had arrived, Daisy was ready to get down to the hard business of carrying out a successful garden show event. Thankful her garden club members were as excited as she was about the upcoming garden show, Daisy was confident the event would be a huge success with local participants.

She had one member of the twenty-member-strong

garden club oversee a specific behind-the-scenes function, twelve major parts in all. Zenith Braxton, a miniature rose buff and Daisy's best friend, was functioning as her assistant by overseeing the various flower show committees in general.

It was up to Zenith to make sure each committee had a responsible chairman and that the duties of each chairman did not overlap. To do this, she maintained constant contact by phone and in person, and, ultimately, she reported what she knew to Daisy. On the actual date of the show, Zenith would stay mobile, free from any specific responsibility other than troubleshooting unexpected problems.

Cinnamon Hartfeld was in charge of the schedule committee, a position that required both focus and strong creative thinking skills. Her primary responsibility was to keep track of general information distributed to the interested public, making sure the rules for each division of the flower show were followed and that the overall flower show was balanced.

Keeping it balanced meant that the various parts of the show were carried out with equal finesse. The flowers used were to be fresh and the right flowers for the season, meaning everything that showed was material that would flourish naturally at this particular time of year.

She made sure that exhibitors were fairly equal in experience, that appropriate space was available for material and for exhibitors and for spectators to move freely between the two. Cinnamon also made sure that the various committees stayed within their budget. Daisy relied on Zenith and Cinnamon the same way she relied on her own two hands: fully aware of their limits and confident in their capabilities.

Whitney Webb functioned as the staging chairman for the garden show and her duties began the moment she first pitched the idea of a garden show to Daisy. Whitney was an experienced gardener who specialized in formal gardens, which she kept in exquisite condition, a result of constant attention to flower head removal, weed control, and constant clipping to achieve the highly manicured look that suited her rather rigid personality.

She was responsible for overseeing stage set-ups and their eventual breakdown, of litter control, lighting, and emergency contingency plans. Whitney was so thorough that she'd submitted a formal drawing of the exhibition site to each committee head, the local police, and fire departments. She had even arranged to have the event videotaped.

Daisy put Mr. Dillingsworth in charge of the judging, which included himself and two other garden club members. He and Kenneth would do any serious lifting that needed to be done before and after the show.

Daisy would handle all publicity, hospitality, and was general girl Friday. She expected record sales at the garden center. She could hardly wait.

Pushing them back and forth in the canopy-covered swing, Kenneth felt her excitement, and even though part of him understood her passion, he also recognized her obsession. More than ever before, he was determined to put romance in the relationship by reminding her at every turn that he was the hard body in her private landscape.

Since meeting Daisy, Kenneth had become increasingly dissatisfied with his Wichita, Kansas, lifestyle. At thirty-eight, he was single, had never been married, and had no children. At six feet two inches tall and two hundred pounds, he was lean, fit, and in his prime, his ebony-colored skin still taut and fit.

His eyes were light brown and friendly. He missed little in the way of details. He distinguished himself among his peers by being both honorable and decisive. He had liked his solitary life just fine until he met Daisy. She had him thinking about organic gardening versus pesticides, watering during the day versus watering at night, and so on.

She made him realize how lonely his life had been, something he discovered when he returned home after meeting her for the first time. His bed, which had once been a source of solace after a long shift at work, had felt empty.

Since then, he'd been to Guthrie as often as time and his schedule permitted, not nearly often enough, which was why he seriously considered Daisy's proposal to work together, but in separate areas of her business. It was crazy enough to work—tiny gazebos for playhouses in a doting mother's backyard.

In the last year, Kenneth had been to Guthrie six times, and Daisy had visited him in Wichita once. He'd been a private investigator for ten years, after a five-year stint with the police department in Wichita, Kansas. He was well trained and well connected. Until recently, he'd been satisfied with his life.

Each time he left Daisy he felt restless, often edgy or even distracted, which in his line of work could easily prove lethal. A change in his lifestyle was necessary, something he was smart enough to realize, but reluctant to act upon without a solid commitment from Daisy.

He was ready to be fully committed to her, yet without the benefit of marriage or even an engagement, the reasonable part of Kenneth's mind didn't think it was wise to chuck a profitable business that was well established for a risky business creating whimsical art for use by Daisy's customers in their gardens.

It was his heart that had no sense of caution. His heart told him to trade his sometimes-dangerous lifestyle for the relaxed social setting that was Daisy's world. In her world, there were no guns or missing persons or long hours spent on surveillance. In her tiny little planet, there was . . . sanctuary, a world within a world.

He loved just thinking about her. At thirty-five, she, too, was single and had never had children. At five feet three inches tall, she was a delightful combination of soft skin and finely tuned muscles that tended to ripple when she walked.

She kept in shape by running with her dog, Cutie Pie, and doing most of the work in her various gardens herself. She generally wore her shoulder-length hair in a ponytail. Her healing spirit and sense of adventure appealed to his own brand of self-containment. Like himself, she was able to create her own system for happiness.

The trouble for Kenneth was that now that his priorities had shifted outward to include her, the issue of their long-distance relationship was a specter before him. It just wasn't practical; it was expensive and tough on them as individuals. He'd think hard about Daisy's proposal. It was either that or nothing at all.

Three

Monday morning

Medium brown, five feet three inches tall, curvy, and casually dressed, fifty-something Rita Rogers adjusted the pageboy wig she'd ordered from the Gold Medal catalog and smiled. She was very pleased with her daughter. In particular, she liked the way Daisy was handling herself during the stress of managing her first garden show, an event Rita hoped would put her daughter on the regional garden map in a big way.

Rita thought it was wonderful that Daisy had a guiding finger in every pie, that she directly handled all major and final decisions, that she was on hand to solve occasional disputes and was responsible for securing and presenting the upcoming awards. Whatever credit came her way as a result of the garden show event would be worthy and appropriate. Rita's face glowed with pride.

To see her child prosper on her own terms filled Rita with a quiet sense of satisfaction. For her, Daisy's success validated whatever sacrifice she'd made in life to be a fair and supportive parent. Rita believed her daughter's outlook was a tribute to her own self-expression and cultural refinement, a marvelous blend of humility and inner strength that had rendered both women beautiful lives. There was much to be thankful for and to appreciate.

"Daisy," Rita said as she settled herself at the kitchen table, coffee mug in hand, "just about everything you touch turns to gold."

Daisy's eyes crinkled at the corners when she smiled. "Only my mother would say what you just did."

Rita swung her gaze to her daughter's left, in order to regard the third person in the room, Kenneth. "I'm not the only one who thinks so. I bet he'd agree."

Sprawled in his chair, his stomach full of tender buttermilk biscuits and sausage gravy, Kenneth clinked coffee mugs with Rita and said, "I definitely do agree."

Daisy changed the subject with a careless wave of her right hand. While it was true that she was sometimes uneasy with compliments, by accepting them without falsely belittling them she was soothed by praise without being spoiled by it. She credited her mother with this ability to stay grounded.

To shift the conversation away from herself, she focused on troubleshooting the garden show. "I'm worried about the level of competition going on between the people who signed up to participate. It's rough."

Kenneth shared her visions of melodrama, and like Daisy he wanted to nip problems before they got out of hand. "I overheard talk of sabotage when I stopped by Gus's Liquor Store to buy some white wine."

Rita's brows rocked up a notch. "Oh, really?"

Kenneth continued. "I heard Miss Myrtle saying to Miss Tilly that Kandi Kane took a bribe by one of the contestants to make her a winner in the garden show."

Daisy laughed in disbelief. She often considered gossip the number-one pastime in Guthrie, sports and religion coming in second and third. "Kandi will be there to report what she finds out. She's not there to judge and she has no way to influence who wins a prize in any of the divisions. There's no reason to bribe her."

Rita refilled their mugs with the last of the coffee. "What if Kandi took money on a job she really can deliver on—like, say, a personal article write-up in her column? It's syndicated across the country. Somebody could potentially get more than fifteen minutes of fame."

Kenneth was shaking his head in bewilderment at the deadly serious way some people were taking what he considered a frivolous function, a show for flowers. He was continually amazed by the differences in his and Daisy's lifestyles, differences that were highlighted by conversations such as this one.

Until meeting Daisy, he'd never given a thought to flowers being grown for exhibition, a hobby he'd discovered appealed to both men and women. He had much to learn in order to keep up with Daisy's constant community involvement. "This is a flower show." He spoke each word with emphasis. "Dirt. Pots. That kind of thing."

Daisy made a face at him. Obviously, he didn't know squat. "Winning first place is a big deal."

Kenneth was determined to be more than the muscle in Daisy's business operation. To do this, he had to be willing to ask the obvious and question the loose ends. How else would he figure out what was going on?

He spoke with care and with patience. "Miss Tilly and Miss Myrtle made it sound like someone's exhibit might be sabotaged in order to make a guaranteed first-place winner." The women were senior members of the garden club who also used the opportunity to give him the questionnaires Daisy would place on the registration table on the day of the garden show. The questionnaire, now stacked on the counter with boxes of black Bic ballpoint pens, was as open and concise as Daisy. The form read:

THANK YOU FOR COMING TO THE FIRST
GUTHRIE FLOWER SHOW
HOSTED BY
DAISY'S ROSE NURSERY AND GARDEN SHOP!

1. *What city and state do you live in?*

_____

2. *Did you have a good time?*

_____

3. *How did you hear about the garden show?*

_____

4. *How old are you? (Please circle one.)*
      20–30   41–50
      31–40   51–up

Comments:

_____

_____

Rita saw him glance at the stack of questionnaires and grabbed one in order to see the finished product. The half sheets of paper were white with bold black print. She said, "In gardening, there are no guarantees. Like this form, it's good to start with the basics and build from there."

"She's got a point," Daisy said. "Given the size of this town and the relatively small scope of the garden show, I agree with you, Mom. Besides," Daisy added with a grin, "in the end, the cheater would never live down the scandal if word of foul play came to light. A contest isn't good unless everybody plays by the same rules."

Kenneth realized Daisy was as competitive as she was practical. He dug for more information. "Tell me about Kandi Kane and her sidekick, Sugar. Are their names for real?" The women, he figured, must have taken a lot of verbal abuse in the form of teasing. He was a firm believer that names contributed to a person's development.

Strong names inspired strength and other names inspired bitterness. Candy and sugar could be both sweet and hard or sweet and soft. Too much of either could make a person sick. A woman might act tough to compensate for the sweet name or she might go with the flow as Daisy had done. Apparently, the snippy-sounding Kandi Kane wasn't sweet and perhaps neither was her daughter, Sugar.

As far as he could tell, Daisy actually fit her name. In nature there were many types of daisies but the one that came to Kenneth's mind had rays of white petals surrounding a disc of yellow, a sturdy and reliable flower that grew freely in the wild or in a gardener's carefully cultivated backyard. In Daisy's backyard, they grew beside her potting shed in huge terra-cotta containers.

She reveled in the dedicated way he embraced her life, as if he wanted to know all the secrets in her gardens, all the quirks that made her uniquely herself. "Yes," she said. "Since the competition was announced eight weeks ago by the garden club, sales have doubled during the week and tripled on the weekend."

Kenneth marveled that Daisy wasn't having performance anxiety. With all the garden show gossip and preevent shenanigans, he was surprised she hadn't put off his visit to Guthrie. Her composure made him feel proud, and like Rita, he smiled. "This Kandi Kane character must really be a celebrity in the garden world."

Rita put her mug on the table hard enough to make it thump against the wood. "She's a regular little bitch, is what she is."

"Mom!"

Rita humphed. "I heard she threw a temper tantrum in Wal-Mart because she had to wait in line like the common Oakie she isn't."

"Is that what she said?" Daisy asked. It always shocked her when high-profile people acted like idiots.

"Yep," Rita said. "Her daughter was reported as saying Kandi ought to be used to Wally World by now."

"Guess so," Daisy said, her manner thoughtful. She figured Kandi's nerves must have been stretched out to the max if she was letting her composure explode in a busy place such as Wal-Mart. The only major shopping place in Guthrie, Wal-Mart for many residents was like the mall.

Clearly, Kenneth didn't have a clue about what Daisy and her mother were saying. "Wally World?" He felt as if he were playing a new board game and was just getting the hang of the rules.

"Around here," Daisy said, "Wal-Mart is often called Wally World."

Kenneth laughed. "I love this town."

Rita cut him a calculated stare. "Why don't you move here? Abe's Real Estate has a house for sale or for rent on my block. It's a two-bedroom single-story bungalow with a detached garage. If you don't like that there's a property with acreage out on Midwest Boulevard that's for sale."

Kenneth surprised Daisy by pumping her mother for more details. "The Midwest Boulevard property is more up my alley. How long has the house been on the market?"

"Less than twenty-four hours," she said. "Sign went up this morning. Wood floors, fresh paint inside and out. No fireplace but lots of windows. No near neighbors and it faces the golf course."

Rita was so happy to finally get a chance to unload her research on house hunting in Guthrie she could scarcely stay in her seat. She was flushed with excitement. As far as she was concerned, Kenneth Gunn would make an excellent son-in-law.

She liked the way he was a thinker and a doer, a combination that made him a successful entrepreneur and private detective. He was the perfect counterpoint to Daisy's feeling-oriented, artistic personality.

By his forming an official, exclusive relationship

with Daisy, Rita figured that Kenneth's presence would keep Daisy from being so totally immersed in her garden center. Unless she was on vacation, Daisy rarely left Guthrie, and when she did, it was seldom beyond the Oklahoma City Metro limits.

Kenneth was fully aware of Rita Rogers's motives. He tapped his left index finger on the table, once, twice. "What Realtor?"

"Lloyd Lentz. Their office is located on Division, right next door to the Walker Tire Company."

Kenneth ignored Daisy's look of chagrin at his continued interest in the property. He couldn't pinpoint its exact location even though he was familiar with the street, a red-dirt-and-rock-covered road that once took him from Guthrie to Edmond on a Sunday-morning drive with Daisy.

On that day, he'd accessed the road off Highway 33, going south on Midwest Boulevard. Along the way, he'd passed a golf course, ranch-styled homes on rural acreage, as well as trailer parks and formal, traditional ranching properties. He was intrigued by the opportunity Rita presented him, one that incorporated his need to be near Daisy and her need to retain autonomy.

"Any way you can get me an appointment to see it?" he asked.

Grinning, Rita also ignored Daisy's surprised expression and wide-open mouth. "I'll get you in there tonight." She pushed her chair away from the table and stood up.

Kenneth understood where Daisy's instant decision-making process came from. Rita didn't waste time with small talk and she wasn't afraid to stick her nose in someone else's business when she felt it was necessary. Apparently, she was worried he and Daisy might not hook up if she didn't put her two cents on the table. "Morning's fine," he said.

Rita slung her purse over her shoulder, its leather soft from constant use and perfectly matched to the custom kangaroo boots she wore with nearly all her casual wear. "Tonight's better," she said, her manner efficient and matter-of-fact. "You can look it over again tomorrow if you like it. If you don't like it, well, then tomorrow you can look at something else."

Kenneth smiled. "I suppose you're right."

Satisfied with her matchmaking skills, Rita bade them both a hasty farewell, but Daisy followed her mother out to her cherry-red vintage sports car with its cream seats and matching rag top. There was no other car like it in Guthrie. The same English rose carved on her boots and purse was also painted on the hood of her car.

"Mom," Daisy said, hands on her hips, "butt out."

Rita never lost stride. She tossed her purse onto the passenger seat, climbed into the car, and pretended her daughter wasn't glaring at her. "You two belong together, Daisy. It would make me very upset if you two didn't stay together because of something as simple as living arrangements. Lots of couples don't live in the same house. Just think of it as a way to keep love new."

Daisy knew all that; she just didn't think her mother should be so pushy. "We're happy the way things are going."

Unperturbed by her daughter's warning tone and look that said "mind your own business," Rita blew her a kiss and turned the key in the ignition. "Love you, too. Ta, ta."

Daisy rolled her eyes and blew a kiss back to her mother. She watched as Rita cut a hard U-turn on the gravel, spun out, then zoomed down the highway as if the speed limit were seventy instead of fifty.

Back in the house, Daisy said, "You don't have to do this, Kenneth." She was embarrassed that he'd been put in a tough predicament.

Kenneth pulled her into his arms and kissed her on the top of her head. "Your mother has too much class to send me out to check on a ramshackle house. We both know this already, so lighten up. Besides, I'm curious."

Daisy squeezed him around the middle. "Me too, I have to admit. I find it interesting the house is available for rent or sale, which keeps your options open."

"Yeah," Kenneth said, his face thoughtful as they returned to their seats at the kitchen table. He'd rinsed the dishes while the women were saying good-bye. "The fact the joint is vacant is what interests me."

"I noticed."

"Know which house it is?"

Daisy threw up her hands in an I-give-up gesture. "Nope. I do know that if you aren't careful, Mom will have you living in that house tomorrow morning and the place furnished by Rent-A-Center before tomorrow night."

Kenneth laughed. He had been in Guthrie enough times to be familiar with the location of major businesses in town. Rent-A-Center was sandwiched between Dollar General and Mega Movies in a convenience strip mall on South Division. "She'll have it accessorized with Wally World decor."

"Mmm-hmm," Daisy said. "She'll have everything

from towels and bedding to bread for the refrigerator and plates for the kitchen cupboards. Anyway, let's get back to Kandi Kane and her daughter, Sugar."

"Go ahead."

"Kandi is a journalist who specializes in the gardening circuit niche. Sugar is her daughter and publicist."

Kenneth tapped a finger on the tabletop twice and then stopped. "The way you say the girl's name makes it sound like she's trouble."

"Sugar tries to be sweet but she really isn't," Daisy said. There was no use trying to be diplomatic. He'd find out anyway.

Kenneth thought about the elderly women he'd run into at Gus's Liquor Store, Miss Myrtle and Miss Tilly. They'd been jazzed, excited about possible fireworks at the garden show. "I'm concerned about all the hotheads."

Daisy sighed hard and rose from the table. "Wait until you meet Kandi. She ought to be here any minute."

A beautiful new Chrysler sedan covered the road at forty miles an hour, ten miles under the posted speed limit on Highway 77 going north toward the center of Guthrie. Kandi Kane checked her lipstick in the rearview mirror, then blew a kiss at her reflection because she looked too damned good in her Velvet Crush lipstick by Maybelline, with its coordinated shades of blush and eye shadow.

Feeling as if she looked good gave her confidence, but being in Guthrie for the garden show brought out the nasty in her. She had an ax to grind in

Guthrie, people to see, to get even with, and the garden show was perfect cover. People had expected her to be rude but they didn't expect her to be rude with an agenda.

She'd been edgy in Wal-Mart, which had done nothing for her private nerves or her public image. Small towns reminded her of the low-key hometown where she'd been raised, and she hated to think of home.

There was no way in the world she'd ever live in a small town again—ever—but no matter how hard she tried to pretend otherwise, Kandi was a small-town girl at heart, a Nebraska farm girl. She'd traveled all over the United States, and despite all the wonderful sights she'd seen, she best enjoyed the open spaces found in rural America, the wildflowers and wild animals, pastures full of goats or sheep or horses or cows. She liked a good thunderstorm, the sound of cicadas at night, the music wind made as it blew through trees and tall grasses, the sight of bright stars in the sky, the clean air and sense of unspoiled innocence that people from large industrial cities called country.

She'd discovered early in her career that life could be a bitch, something she believed in after she divorced her husband. She hadn't lived in a small town since, nor had she ever married again. She thought marriage was for suckers.

Kandi's best asset from her marriage was the creation of her only child, Sugar, a young woman who had grown into someone both bitter and sweet, like a chocolate best suited for baking instead of eating right out of a silver foil wrapper, Hershey's Kisses style.

She spoke to her reflection. "Today, we're gonna get even."

At the sight of the sign saying DAISY'S ROSE NURSERY AND GARDEN SHOP, she flashed her signal to turn right. The property was composed of rustic and weathered buildings surrounded by gardens so lavish it was hard for Kandi to believe most everything was for sale or that she was in farm country.

Daisy's roses were not squashed together; they were grouped by color and laid out in half-crescent shapes with a walking path for customers to use while browsing.

The business was separated from the house by a grove of redbud trees and a deep green lawn. There was a privacy hedge composed of Siberian elm kept trimmed to roughly twelve feet. On the south side of the elm fence was the business; on the north side was Daisy's personal residence.

To the untrained eye, Daisy's private garden was a continuation of the nursery and garden shop, but to Kandi's professional eye, there was an exquisite sense of order about the garden that made Kandi, despite her garden expertise, feel welcome and pleased. Daisy's private gardens enticed the senses and soul, so that when Kandi pulled into the drive she sighed with relief.

Her car, with its glossy surface and sleek lines, looked out of place next to Daisy's dusty work truck with its load of decorative red native sandstone in the back. Idly, Kandi wondered if the stone would be used in Daisy's home or in her business. For the first time in a long time, Kandi felt like getting her hands dirty with actual yard work.

It had been a long time since she'd worn a pair of

faded jeans and rubber gardening boots. It was 12:00—high noon. The sun was so hot, Kandi felt as if its heat was melting all the tension from her body.

There was no breeze, and yet the presence of Daisy's gardens had the effect of cool running water. Lush green foliage, vibrant reds and purples and pinks in flowers so strong and beautiful Kandi felt a surprise surge of delight and anticipation that she would be a key factor in Daisy Rogers's first garden show, but when Kandi remembered her true reason for accepting the invitation to attend the exhibition, a shadow darkened her features and brought a scowl to her face.

Daisy opened her front door and was not surprised to see the ugly look on Kandi's face. The woman was always scowling, always dissatisfied about something, if what was said in the press was true. Daisy threw an extra watt into her smile. "It's great to see you, Kandi. Come on in."

Kandi really wanted a tour of the gardens. Her tone was arrogant even though she didn't mean to be rude. "Where exactly will the exhibition take place?" She hadn't meant to skip the small talk, either, and realized how poorly she presented herself to her casually dressed hostess.

Daisy hadn't expected any other type of behavior. She didn't mind sticking to business. "At the fairgrounds." Her tone was cordial.

"On Division?"

"Yes."

"It's amazing how much I remember about this place," Kandi said as her eyes searched the quiet. "Haven't been here since my daughter graduated from Langston two years ago."

"There's been a lot of changes in town since then."

Kandi's laugh was genuine and surprised them both. "I saw some of them, like the Fleetwood homes on Industrial and Division, the new storage place next to Roller World. By the way, I can't believe the roller rink is really a bingo parlor. Why can't the bingo people get their own place around here?"

"Good question," Daisy said, her brows tilted at a how-should-I-know angle. "Would you like me to show you around the gardens?"

"Please."

Kandi looked as relieved as she felt. This was one occasion when she would enjoy the behind-the-scenes activities associated with being a keynote speaker at a public gardening event. In a larger city, they might have met in a restaurant to run over the details of the show, but in this small-town arena, the professional edge was less cutthroat and more humanity based.

In this instance, Kandi knew she was being treated to a rare insider's view of Daisy's passion for gardening. The experience was similar to a bookworm visiting another bookworm's private library. When Kandi spoke, her gratitude and pleasure were genuine. "I'd like that. Thank you."

"You're welcome."

Kandi was older than Daisy by twenty-two years but she looked every bit as healthy and alive as Daisy did. The most significant contrast between them stemmed from the aura they presented.

Kandi was serious, forceful, dynamic in her beauty. She was five feet six inches tall, carried her weight well, looked as if she exercised on a regular basis. She was manicured, from her hair to the French pedicure on her clipped and pampered toes.

Her clothes were loose and free on her body, the tropical-colored fabric lightweight and as obviously expensive as the understated perfume she wore and the close-cropped precision cut on her head.

Daisy was open, friendly, charismatic, a universally attractive woman, universal because she appealed equally to men and women, both sexes drawn to her easygoing manner. Her dress reflected her present state of mind.

She wore navy capri pants with a pale green tank top, a straw hat, and green gardening clogs. The image she presented was one of a young woman strolling through a meadow with a basket of fresh-cut flowers carried in the crook of one arm as she made her way to the potting shed in order to arrange them.

The women crossed the gravel on the ground in front of Daisy's house and met Kenneth part way in his approach. A healthy man in his physical prime, he looked as if he didn't have a care in the world, as if his entire being was centered and his future was not only known but on track, his master-life design the perfect complement to his personality.

Kandi was astute enough to notice that Kenneth's self-assuredness matched Daisy's composure in parallel lines and that together they made a formidable couple. She admired their obvious rightness and unity together.

On the short walk to Daisy's front door, Kandi cataloged the minutiae of her immediate view: the slate color of the gravel, the tenacity of volunteer elm trees growing between cobbled flagstones.

She noticed a crumbly dirt mixture and knew immediately that the mound she saw was the final stage of a compost pile. The compost was situated next to a roughly four-foot-tall greenhouse made of glass. Inside the glass structure were assorted plants in small pots, mostly seedlings and herbs.

Again, Kandi had the urge to throw on some jeans and rubber gardening shoes in order to explore the visual treats in Daisy's gardens. They were as friendly and inviting as the woman who'd created them.

With effort, Kandi reminded herself of the true purpose she had in accepting Daisy's invitation: revenge. It was too bad Daisy and her lover would play a part in her own personal drama. Kandi shrugged once more. As far as she was concerned, casualties existed in every war, especially those between friends and business relationships.

Inside the house, she noticed the German shepherd. "Big dog you've got there." She said it with the cautious respect a large dog generates in people who don't know it. The dog flicked her tail twice but made no move to sniff or otherwise investigate Kandi.

Daisy eyed her seventy-five-pound canine with affection. "Her name is Cutie Pie." Quiet in general, loyal as a rule, the German shepherd was Daisy's secret weapon. If the dog ever thought her owner was in danger, she switched from friendly calm to deadly adversary in less time than it took to blink.

Kandi snorted in disbelief. "If you say so."

In her book, Cutie Pie was a fit name for a toy poodle. This dog had the regal bearing of a queen and the watchful gaze of a trained soldier. With the shepherd around, Kandi doubted anyone would get ideas about raiding Daisy's home while she was working in the garden shop. Cutie Pie had the power and mind-set to chew up a trespasser and leave him for Daisy to find in the driveway. Kenneth Gunn and Cutie Pie made excellent protectors.

Kandi felt a stab of envy. This was one of those odd occasions when she wished she'd chosen a more tra-ditional path for herself. She had a gorgeous home, a carefully constructed career, but she lacked true qual-ity in her private life, such as treasured friends and other gratifying relationships.

In Daisy's kitchen, cream Formica counters were adorned with white appliances, and clearly, the most commonly used appliance of all was the twelve-cup coffeepot, currently filled with fresh brew. The white theme brought to mind a cleanness and purity of spirit that served to make Daisy's home a non-threatening place to be. Kandi was struck by the wholesome, balanced part of her hostess's creative spirit. To drink coffee in this setting was like drink-ing happiness from the bowl of a clean ceramic cup in an open room filled with the soothing light of friendship.

Beside the coffeepot was a stainless-steel coffee grinder and several clear jars of whole coffee beans. The labels on the jars read *Henry's, Post Alley Decaf, Taza Doro Espresso,* and *Seattle's Best.* "I love this coffee," she said, her eyes lit up.

"Me, too," Daisy said. "I get it right here in town."

Daisy's come-what-may attitude soothed Kenneth as much as it did Kandi, who sat at the kitchen table with her shoes kicked off and her nose held over the steam rising from the cup she held in her man-icured hands.

Kenneth understood Kandi's immediate sense of

welcome and relaxation because he'd felt the same way when he first sat at Daisy's table. Then, he'd been physically injured and suffering from amnesia. Her no-nonsense attitude, reflected in her kitchen decor, had helped him deal with the pain and suffering he experienced over being beaten and left for dead on her property.

Daisy's nails weren't polished like Kandi's—they were chipped on two fingers—and yet it was from those caring hands that the wonderful, fresh-ground coffee was made, as was the lush garden view from the windows in her quiet kitchen, the sound of birds outside serving as background music.

For the second time since waking up with Daisy that morning, Kenneth felt blessed to be a part of her life. Her mother's suggestion to relocate to Guthrie for good was very appealing, especially during nearly spiritual, entirely uplifting moments like these.

As Daisy and Kandi discussed the flower show, he allowed himself to fully unwind, his mind registering the even rhythm of Daisy's words the way he might assimilate the sound of some type of healing music, the sound of wind or sea during moments of calm.

Kandi's presence was the only discordant note in the bucolic setting. Kandi, with her sleek car and her chic look and her history of nastiness and aggression. Those were not qualities found in Daisy's basic personality or her living environment.

There was an odd sort of quiet going on as they all shared coffee together. It was, for Kenneth, much like riding on an airplane with strangers who were content to be silent, people who were not compelled to talk to neighbors in order to pass time. Instead they slept or read or meditated, eyes focused casually into space.

Almost idly, Kenneth glanced at Kandi Kane and wondered if she would prove to be the storm after all the calm in Daisy's kitchen. He pushed away the thought, focused on nothing particular, his eyes touching everything around him as he evaluated the decision to move to Guthrie in order to be near Daisy full-time.

Like Kandi did, he thought her kitchen was descriptive of her style of living. The kitchen was highly efficient, with little clutter. The center cooking island and convenience sink were as neat as the countertops. Cookbooks were lined up beside books on growing herbs and making skin care products from the bounty of her tiny kitchen garden.

There were small pots of living plants, nothing fancy, but the fact the greenery was healthy and thriving showed Daisy's care for the simplest aspects of gardening as much as she did the larger ones, like growing companion plants to sell with the roses in her commercial gardens. The Russell lupines in purples and blues had become his favorites.

"Hey," Daisy said, "Kenneth?"

He laughed a little self-consciously. "Daydreaming."

Kandi eyed him with open speculation. "Some private eye you are. I thought you all were edgy, cigarette-smoking, whiskey-drinking, live-on-the-edge kind of guys. You look like a corporate dot-com exec of some type."

Kenneth appraised Kandi just as coldly, but unlike hers, his tone was neither here nor there, it was entirely neutral. "Don't bite your tongue."

It was obvious to Daisy, Kandi wasn't sure if she'd

been insulted or invited to further speak her mind. She decided to take control of the conversation by putting an end to it. "Kandi, I'm sure you're tired and will want to rest at your hotel. Call me in the morning and we'll get together for lunch."

Kandi gave her a give-me-a-break look. "Don't try to manipulate me. I'll go when I'm good and ready."

This, Kenneth decided, was the Kandi that Daisy had warned him about. He wrestled Kandi's attention away from their hostess. "I'll walk you to your car."

Kandi seldom argued with handsome men, especially young handsome men like Kenneth. Tension fell away from her face with the ease of a seasoned actress, which is exactly what she was being at that particular moment. Her problem was that she didn't feel like driving all the way to Edmond after winding down at Daisy's.

If she'd known she'd be this at ease after her meeting, she would have stayed at Amy's Place on the corner of Vilas and First Street, just three miles away from Daisy's house, instead of driving the twenty miles to the Ramada Inn. Amy's Place, a bed-and-breakfast that specialized in everything from facials to full-body massage and reflexology, would have been the perfect way to cap off the last hour she'd spent with Daisy and Kenneth.

"You're right," she said. "I am tired." She gathered her purse and shoved her feet back into shoes that were so tight they made her toes hurt. Still, despite her snippy remarks, Kandi had made herself a much-sought-after commodity by being all vinegar and a little salt. Salt was a natural preservative.

She used just enough salt in her conversation to guarantee a listener's attention but not so much salt she repeatedly spoiled public taste for the words she cooked up in her syndicated writing column on gardening. There was never a viable substitute for honest and true good manners. She used them to say, "Thanks for the coffee and the tour."

Those were the last kind words she'd ever have to say to anyone.